# LIFE
# SAFARI

# Other Works
# by John P. Strelecky

*The Why Café* (www.whycafe.com)

*Big Five for Life*™ - (CD Series - www.bigfiveforlife.com)

*The Big Five for Life – Leadership's Greatest Secret*
(www.bigfiveforlife.com)

*How to be Rich and Happy*
(www.howtoberichandhappy.com)

**More information about other works
by the author can be found at:
www.thelifesafari.com**

# LIFE
## SAFARI

*John P. Strelecky*

**Aspen Light Publishing**

ISBN: 978-0-9834896-0-3

Aspen Light Publishing Paperback edition 2011
Aspen Light Publishing Hardcover edition 2007

For information address:
Aspen Light Publishing
13506 Summerport Village Parkway #155
Windermere, Florida 34786

The author can be reached at: jstrelecky@bigfiveforlife.com or through
www.thelifesafari.com

Printed in U.S.A

# Acknowledgements

To Africa, and all those who make her their home.
To my wife, Xin, *you* are my home.
To my daughter, Sophia, you make my heart smile.
To my parents, for teaching me the joy of travel.
To Oprah, for pushing me to think bigger, and do more.

*A special thanks to Tricia Crisafulli for her tremendous passion and enthusiasm for this story, to Doris Michaels and Delia Berrigan Fakis, of the DSM Literary Agency for all their assistance, and to Matt Blauvelt, Patrick O'Connor, Kristen Manieri, Carol Jose, and Brad Borchers for their insights and inspiration.*

*"There is a place inside our soul where we hold our greatest wishes. Those wishes are our Big Five for Life."*

—Ma Ma Gombe

# 1

I picked up the leather-bound notebook that had been my constant companion throughout the journey. The pages were weather-beaten and torn from the effects of rain and sun and the sheer challenges that came with crossing a continent on foot.

Much had transpired since then, but each time I held that journal I was instantly transported back. And each time, the memory began the same way, with my entrance into Africa.

How long ago that seemed, and yet how powerful was the experience—powerful enough that it has remained a permanent part of my soul. After all, I almost died there. After all, I found my life there.

I didn't know what to expect when I began my journey to Africa. Other than pictures I had seen in books, I knew almost nothing about the people, the animals, or the environment I would encounter. But at the time, none of that seemed to matter. I knew one thing, and that one thing was enough. I knew I needed to be happy. For some reason, I thought Africa was the

place where I would find my happiness.

I opened the journal. There it was: *Day 1.* I had noted it as such with a single statement. "Today, the adventure begins." And indeed it had. I crossed to Africa by ship. The journey took the better part of three weeks. When I left home, I carried nothing more than a large backpack full of clothes, basic camping supplies, good hiking boots, an oversized hat to protect myself from the sun, and the money I'd saved over the course of two years.

Two years was the time it took me to go from the start of my dream to the beginning of my reality. Two years may seem like a long time to wait to pursue one's dream, but not when compared to the lifetime most people spend. Many a person during those two years had expressed how they also would love to go to Africa. Initially I tried to explain that if I could do it so could they. I certainly wasn't the highest paid person among them. As a matter of fact, I was probably one of the lowest.

But I soon realized that they weren't truly serious about going to Africa, or else they would be going. They liked to talk about their dreams, but in the end, they just left them as dreams. They didn't know what I had felt a glimpse of, and what Ma Ma Gombe would confirm for me. That dreams are in fact realities waiting to happen. But they don't wait forever. At some point you have to help them make the transition. Or eventually, they just fade away.

So there I stood, a six-foot-one-inch, twenty-two-year-old kid. Having been an athlete most of my life, I was relatively lean but muscular. To a stranger I would have seemed quietly confident without being cocky—a little unsure of my future and yet hopeful that I was heading in the right direction.

My ancestors had come from Eastern Europe, and I'd inherited the genes of a mix of nations. My blonde hair and blue eyes were like my mother's, my ability to tan quickly to a deep brown hue reflected more of my father's family.

And there I was—in Africa.

# 2

My first step onto the African continent was not as exciting as I'd imagined it would be. I don't know why, but for some reason I never pictured walking off the boat and into a *town*. Logically that would have made sense, but for some reason when I'd thought of Africa, I'd envisioned open plains of incomparable beauty and countless animals. I would find that, as it would turn out, just not at the boat dock.

When I stepped off the gangplank, I was greeted by throngs of people. Countless black faces inquiring if I needed a guide, transportation, a place to stay, something to eat... I declined each of their invitations and made my way into town. Prior to leaving my own country, I'd read that the best place for travelers to stay was a small hotel called The Escape.

I had been instantly drawn to it, simply because of the name. I was trying to escape, so where better to escape to than a hotel of the same name. It took me twenty minutes of walking through the narrow streets before I found the hotel. Had I

known where I was going, it probably would have been a five minute journey, but I was a little lost and also captivated by all that I saw around me.

The streets were a bustle of activity, with meat vendors selling large pieces of soft-skinned animals such as Impala and Kudu. The meat had been cut and dried, and now the vendors had it displayed on tables in the hot sun. Other merchants hawked camping supplies, safari equipment, guns, machetes, maps, and oddities such as animal horns and hooves. The town was organized chaos, with travelers outlining their journeys and guides gathering supplies.

When I arrived at the hotel I could see why it had been recommended. It wasn't that it was posh or expensive. Instead, its beauty came from the nature around it. The owner had integrated lush gardens in front and out back, with the spectacular views of the mountains to the North. That plus the use of local wood carvings created what for a better term, looked like an excellent "Escape."

I walked through the wide open door and up to the front desk. Behind the counter, a man dressed in khaki clothing turned from his book and looked up at me. "Good morning, mate," he said and smiled. "What can I do for you?"

"I heard that this was the best place in town to stay for a while and get your bearings before heading out," I responded.

"Right, well, that's what we shoot for," he said and smiled again.

"My name is Jack," I said and extended my hand.

"Pleasure, Jack, I'm Mick."

"Where you from Mick?" I asked as we shook hands.

"All kinds of parts, really. I was born in Australia, but this has been home for the last 10 years more or less. Before that it was Asia for a while, and South America before that."

I nodded.

"What brings you to Africa, Jack?" he asked.

"That's a good question," I thought. "I don't know exactly. I just felt a pull of some kind to come here. So I saved up for two years and now, here I am."

"Right, well, when in doubt, go with your gut," he said and smiled once more. "Most people come to see the animals, does that interest you?"

I nodded, "That's a big part of what I want to experience."

"What types of animals are you hoping to get a look at?"

"I suppose all of them would seem a bit broad, but really, I want to see as many types as I can," I replied. "Elephants, rhinos, lions, leopards, buffalo, antelope, hippos… All of them."

"Well, the first five you named are referred to around here as the African Big Five," Mick explained. "You'll need a guide for that. Actually you'll need a guide for everything except zebra

and antelope. Those you can see if you just wander to the top of the big plateau out back and look in the opposite direction of the ocean. That whole savannah out there is full of them."

"You're kidding."

"Nope, not at all," he replied.

"Is it dangerous?"

"Nah, not really. There aren't many lions in this area anymore."

"Why do I need a guide to see the other animals?"

"Well, you could wing it on your own, but heading out on safari isn't like going to the zoo. Some of the animals only live in certain parts of the country, so you'll have to travel a good distance if you want to see them all. And you have to know what you're looking for. Like I said, it isn't like going to a zoo. Then there's always the possibility you'll get attacked by something. Better to be with someone who knows what they're doing."

"How much of a distance are we talking about?" I asked.

"Well, on foot, it could take you months, maybe even a year to see it all. The upside of that is you really get to experience Africa. Otherwise you could use horses, or take boats to different ports and enter from there. That would definitely cut down your time. How long do you have here?"

"As long as it takes," I replied. "I quit my job back home, sold almost everything, and put the few remaining things in storage. I guess I've got as long as it takes until I run out of money."

"Then I'd walk," he suggested. "If you're here to see it and experience it, might as well see it and experience it. That will keep your costs low too."

I wasn't really excited by the idea of walking for a year, but I didn't want to shut down my options until I understood them better. "So where do I find a guide, Mick? And do any of them speak English?"

"Ask around as you're meeting people in town. I'll keep my ears open too. Now that I know what you're looking for, it shouldn't be too hard to find someone who's heading out soon. Yours is going to be a bit longer of a trip, so it may take a while, but we should be able to find someone.

"Regarding English, most people here are bilingual. They all speak their own language and then some English too. A leftover influence from when the Brits were here."

I nodded slowly, taking in all that he'd explained. "You mentioned earlier that I could see some zebra and antelope somewhere nearby, right?"

"Sure, just head out to that giant plateau you see off to the north. It takes about an hour-and-a-half to get from here to the top. There's a pretty well-marked game trail, just follow that. You thinking of going today?" he asked.

"Yeah, from what you've just shared it sounds like I've got a few things to contemplate. Seems like a good place to do that."

# 3

An hour later I was more than halfway to the top of the plateau. As I walked, I could see herds of zebra and antelope grazing in the grasses below. It seemed surreal. I was in Africa.

I didn't pass any other people during my hike. The Escape was on the very outskirts of the town, and all the activity was between it and the docks. Out here was wilderness—pristine, beautiful, and wide open wilderness.

When I reached the top, I found a small shade tree to sit beneath. Then I alternated between marveling at the animals on the plains below and capturing my thoughts in my journal. Before leaving on my trip I'd purchased a brown, leather-bound journal. I hadn't known what to expect of my travels, but it seemed like a worthy item to bring along.

Thanks to a combination of the warm breezes, the quiet environment, and fatigue from my travels, I dozed off. When I woke up, I was startled to see an old woman sitting a few feet away. Hearing me awaken, she turned and smiled at me.

Her hair was almost completely white from age. She had dark brown skin, and eyes that danced with life.

"Did you have a nice rest?" she asked in British style English that was flavored with an African accent.

"Yes," I replied, and tried to transition from asleep to awake. My head felt groggy and I was surprised at having someone sitting next to me.

"I understand you are looking for a guide," she said.

"Yes, I am. I want to see the animals. Do you know someone who can take me?"

"I thought perhaps I could take you," she said, and smiled again.

I didn't know what to say without appearing ungrateful. She was obviously very old, and although she looked healthy, she was very thin. I doubted she could last a few weeks of traveling, let alone many months, or even a year, as Mick had indicated.

"You're a guide?" I asked, trying to keep the doubt from my voice.

"Yes," she replied slowly. "I am a guide. My name is Gombe Narubu. People call me Ma Ma Gombe."

I rose and walked the few feet to where she was sitting. "My name is Jack. It's a pleasure to meet you, Ma Ma Gombe."

"And it is a pleasure to meet you, young Jack."

She paused and looked into my eyes, "Although you are not

so young in your soul as you appear on the outside, are you?" she asked.

I looked at her, perplexed, "I'm not sure what you mean."

She smiled and slightly nodded her head a few times, "You will. Why are you here in Africa, young Jack?"

I shifted my gaze out to the waving grass and grazing animals. "I don't know exactly. I was struggling to find my place back home. I was struggling to find what made me happy. My whole life I have dreamed of seeing the animals in Africa, and so without knowing what else to do, I focused on that. Now I'm here."

"Good for you," she said. "Most people don't get that far with their dreams."

I turned and faced her, "And you, what brings you to this particular place?"

She hesitated for a moment, and looked into my eyes again. "I am here because you and I were supposed to meet," she replied. "I am here because I believe that your Big Five for Life and mine are connected."

I gave her another confused look, "Big Five? Is that related to the African Big Five? The guy at my hotel told me that's the name people here use for elephant, leopard, lion, buffalo, and rhinoceros."

"Everything is related, young Jack. Everything is connected.

Yes, in the same way that visitors to Africa seek to see the African Big Five, so they feel their safari experience was a success, so too can people seek their own Big Five, so that they see their *life* as a success."

I looked out again at the sea of grass beneath me, waving in the gentle breeze. "I wouldn't know much about that. Success is something I have struggled with."

"Perhaps that is because you have not found your own Big Five for Life yet," she replied softly.

There was something very likeable about Ma Ma Gombe. The youthfulness in her eyes, and her calming presence, gave her the aura of a learned soul, a wise woman—someone who had seen much in her life and had grown because of it.

Ma Ma Gombe got up from her seat on the ground. "You have just arrived, young Jack. I will give you time to rest. Tomorrow afternoon I will be here again. We can talk more then."

And with that, she was gone. I moved back to my original position at the base of the tree and leaned my back up against it.

"There's no way she could be my guide," I thought. "She's old, she's so small, and she doesn't even wear a hat. How can you be an African guide without wearing a hat?"

# 4

"None of them wear hats," Mick said as he poured me a drink at the bar. "I mean the Westerners do, but not the Africans. They've grown up with the sun, they don't need hats. They don't have light eyes like you and me, which require shading to be able to see. They don't need to cover themselves from the sun either. They are perfectly in sync with their environment. None of them wear hats."

"Ok, so they don't wear hats. How about her age? I mean, how old is Ma Ma Gombe?"

"Jack, listen. I understand where you're coming from on this. An outsider sees Ma Ma Gombe and thinks, no way can that old woman guide me across Africa. But the fact of the matter is, I would take her as my guide more than any other person in this town.

"I couldn't believe it when she walked in here this afternoon. It hadn't been more than a couple of hours after we talked about what you wanted to do, and how you needed a guide, and then

there she is. Let me tell you something else, she wasn't even shocked when I told her you had just arrived. I don't know how she does it, but she just seems to know these things."

"Mick, I'm not doubting you. You've been here ten years, and if you say she's a great guide, then I believe you, but what about safety. I mean, I'm guessing she doesn't carry a gun right? What happens if we get out there and get in trouble?"

Mick smiled, "Maybe that's what makes her such a good guide. She doesn't get people into places that *are* trouble. Remember this morning when I talked about going with someone who knows what they're doing? Trust me, Ma Ma Gombe definitely knows what she's doing."

I looked at him, still doubtful.

"Jack, if you had told me you wanted to do a two to four week excursion on horses, where you would be traipsing around everywhere and stirring things up in the bush, I would recommend someone else. But if you really want to experience Africa, this is a once in a lifetime chance. Ma Ma Gombe *is* old, and who knows how many more trips she'll take.

"She has walked this continent, my friend. She's part of this place, and it's a part of her. She knows things that all the other guides combined don't understand. And from what she told me, this trip has special meaning to her. I think you'd be crazy to pass up this opportunity."

He paused and looked at me. "I'll tell you one other thing about Ma Ma Gombe," Mick continued. "She understands the energy of Africa."

"What does that mean?" I asked.

"There is a rhythm to this place," he explained. "It's similar to what I've felt back home in the Outback. People who can tap into that rhythm are never truly in danger. It may not always seem that way, but it's true. They know what's coming before it even gets there. Ma Ma Gombe is tapped into that rhythm."

That night before I went to sleep, I stood in the lobby of The Escape. For the first time since my arrival, I acknowledged something. It was the energy Mick had talked about. In the air was a sensation of excitement so thick, that it practically screamed at you. This was a leaping off point for adventure. I could sense it. I could feel it on my skin.

"Maybe Mick is right about Ma Ma Gombe after all," I said to myself.

# 5

"They are the five things you want to do, see, or experience in your lifetime before you die, young Jack—the five things that if you did, saw, or experienced them, you would consider your life to be a success as you have defined success. They are not about what your parents think, or your neighbors think, or your boss, family, or even spouse thinks. This is about what you think."

I leaned back against the tree as I listened to Ma Ma Gombe. It was late in the afternoon and the sun was finally starting to cool down. I had climbed to the top of the plateau and once again fallen asleep under the tree. And once again, Ma Ma Gombe had been there when I awoke. She was now explaining to me what she meant the day before with the Big Five for Life.

"I've never heard of this before," I said.

"That does not surprise me," she replied. "Not many people have."

"So why are you explaining it to me?" I asked.

"I told you yesterday that we are all connected, young Jack.

Do you remember that?"

"Yes."

"I believe you and I are more connected than either one of us may realize. I believe our paths have crossed so that we can help each other fulfill part of our own Big Five for Life."

"I see," I replied, then shook my head. "No, I don't see. I thought you were interested in being my guide. What does that have to do with my Big Five for Life? And what does it have to do with yours."

Ma Ma Gombe touched my shoulder. "Look," she said and pointed to the plains below. "How important is it for you to walk out there, to see those animals up close, to experience Africa?"

I followed the direction of her finger and was instantly as captivated by the zebra and antelope as I had been the moment I saw them the day before.

"It's very important," I replied.

"You told me you worked for two years to save enough money to come here," she said. "Would you say that at this moment in your life, it's so important that it is one of the five most important things you want to do, see, or experience before you die."

"Yes," I replied.

"Then that is your connection. You are here to experience one of your Big Five for Life, although you did not even know it before you arrived. And I am here to guide you through that."

"And how am I connected to your Big Five for Life?" I asked.

"I do not know for sure," she replied. "But I think that will become more apparent as we go. For now, let me share with you that I have just one of my Big Five for Life left.

"Since I was a child, I have dreamed of going to a place my grandfather used to call 'the birthplace of all.' When he was a young man he visited there. And when I was a little girl he used to tell me that it is a place where you can watch life awaken as the sun rises in the east, and watch the world go to sleep, when the sun sets in the west.

"I have dreamed of it my entire life, and I believe that I shall go soon."

"And how am I connected to that?" I asked.

"I do not know, young Jack. Perhaps in no other way than what you pay me for guiding you, I will use to go there. Perhaps there is more. That is part of what we shall find out, won't we?"

She patted my leg. "I will show you Africa, young Jack. I will show you her animals, her people, her natural beauty. I will help you fulfill that part of your Big Five for Life. As for the connection to my Big Five for Life, that we will uncover along the way."

I had no idea all that I was getting into when I agreed to Ma Ma Gombe's offer. At the time it seemed potentially crazy, and yet somehow, impossible to refuse. My decision proved to be a wise one, for had I not decided as I did—it would have been the biggest mistake of my life.

# 6

We were on the road less than a day and already it had become apparent what an asset Ma Ma Gombe was. Before we left, she took me to the market in town. With the precision of a diamond cutter, she had selected what we needed for our travels. We carried only the most essential items. Everything else was left unpurchased, or in the case of many items from my backpack, they were left behind.

Everyone knew Ma Ma Gombe, and there was an unusual energy to her interactions. With each person we met, she explained that we were embarking on a journey to fulfill parts of our Big Five for Life. They in turn took a deeper level of interest in everything we were doing, and each item we purchased. More than one merchant gave us superior items for no greater cost. And each was as meticulous in their evaluation of their goods, as if they themselves were going on the journey.

I asked Ma Ma Gombe about that on the first day of our travels.

"It is a strange paradox of life, young Jack. People want to be part of something amazing. When they know that you are fulfilling part of your Big Five for Life—part of what will define your life as a success or not—they want to be a part of that too. Did you see the care with which the merchants went through their items?"

"I did," I replied. "Everything was tested three times and practically gift wrapped. I've never seen people so interested in making sure I was going to be successful."

"Yes," she said. "People will often do more for others than they will for themselves. I read a book once about a very famous man. He did a study to find out how connected we all are. The study included an experiment where he sent a package to a person in a particular town. Along with the package, he included a note explaining to the recipient that the goal was to get the package hand-delivered to someone in another town that was very, very far away.

"The original person who received the item could only give it to someone they knew on a first-name basis, someone who they felt would either be going to the other town, or who would know someone who was going to the other town.

"The man doing the study wanted to know how many people the package would be passed to before it was hand-delivered to the town that was far away."

"What did he find?" I asked.

"He found two things. First of all, he found that only six people separated the two strangers. Second, and this is equally important, he found that the single greatest factor in whether someone would deliver the package or not, was the perceived value of the package.

"If they thought it had a high value, they were very likely to help. If they thought it had a low value, they often did not help. The reason you saw the vendors demonstrate such meticulous care when they were helping us, is because we are pursuing our Big Five for Life. Our 'package' is one of the five things that if we do, see, or experience it, then our lives will be a success as we have defined success."

"That has a high value?" I asked.

"The highest."

And as it went with the vendors on that first day, so would it go throughout our journey. No matter the size of the village, or status of the stranger, each went to extraordinary lengths to help us achieve the success we had defined for ourselves.

# 7

By our third day of walking, we had left all signs of civilization behind. It was an endless sea of waving yellow grass, interrupted in brief intervals by trees of a sort I had never seen before. Ma Ma Gombe explained to me that they were Baobab trees.

"They are God's reminder to find laughter in the world, young Jack. When God planted the Baobab trees, he put them with the roots sticking out, so that no matter how tiring the journey, a traveler would see them and be reminded of the laughter in life."

And it was true. The trees had massive thick trunks that supported a spindly array of branches which really did look like roots. They were captivating.

As we traveled, Ma Ma Gombe made a point of showing me plants and explaining what they were used for. Some could be made into medicines. Others could be dug from deep in the ground and softened over a flame to eat. One particular root provided enough sustenance for an entire day of walking.

She also taught me to read the weather and the behavior of

the animals. We had already seen hundreds of zebras, antelope, and families of warthogs during our journey. With each animal we passed, she would point out their nuances. How a particular gazelle would turn one ear in one direction and the other ear in the opposite direction, thereby listening simultaneously to all that was going on.

Or the way the animals would spread out in a herd. Each facing a different direction so that collectively they could smell a predator from miles away, no matter which way the predator came from.

She didn't just explain things either. She would question me on what she shared, to make sure I understood it. As I would realize later, there was a reason she wanted me to not only understand these things, but to *know* them.

It was like going to school in the greatest university ever created. Each day was a new and exciting lesson in the way the world worked.

For the first few days of our journey, I found myself constantly wondering how far we were going to walk that day. Each time I asked Ma Ma Gombe, she replied "until we stop." On the fourth day, when I once again asked her, Ma Ma Gombe turned to me and smiled. "Young Jack, why is it that you are always concerned about how far we are going to walk?"

"I don't know," I replied. "I guess I like to keep track of how

we're doing—whether we're on time or not."

Ma Ma Gombe extended her arms wide and looked around at the open plains. "And if we are not?" she asked. "And on whose schedule are we walking? Young Jack, do you see that buzzard?"

She pointed to the south where a large buzzard was circling slowly in the sky. "Do you think he is always thinking about whether he is on time or not? He knows that when he is hungry and the lion has made a kill, he needs to move as quickly as possible. And when there is no kill to scavenge from, or when his belly is full, he simply needs to be. Nothing more, nothing less.

"If we are always worrying about what is coming next, we sacrifice the chance to interact with everything that is going on around us. We can never get to the future, young Jack. When we arrive there, it is no longer the future; it becomes the present. So we can either enjoy life as it happens, or we can always be getting ready to enjoy it."

Ma Ma Gombe smiled at me. "Let me tell you a story," she began. "When I was a child, my brothers and I used to play a game. We would take a stick and place it in the ground. Then we would take a hoop made of woven grass and try to throw it so that it fell over the stick. We would each take ten tries and the one who had thrown the hoop over the stick the most times was the winner.

"I am the only girl in my family and the youngest child on

top of that. My brothers were always stronger and faster. But in this game I could hold my own. I would focus very hard on each throw, and more often than not, I was the winner. The problem was that I did not enjoy the game. It took so much of my energy to focus on each throw, that the only moment I enjoyed was when the last hoop had landed and I was the winner.

"One day my grandfather saw me sitting by myself and he came up to me. 'Little Gombe,' he asked, 'why are you not playing with your brothers? They are playing with the hoop and stick. I thought you loved that game.'

"'No grandpa,' I told him. 'I only love winning. The rest of it is very tiring. I have to focus so hard on throwing the hoop each time, that it is no longer fun except when I win. And when I win, we just start a new game right away, so the feeling of winning only lasts a little while.'

"He picked me up and put me on his lap. 'Little Gombe, perhaps you need to play the game a different way.'

"'What do you mean, grandpa?' I asked him.

"'Well, you like the feeling when you win, don't you?'

"I nodded and told him, yes."

"'Well, why don't you feel that way every time you throw the hoop and it goes over the stick?' he asked me. 'If winning provides a moment of joy, then with the way you play now, the most you can have is one moment of joy—and that is only if you win.

But if you feel a moment of joy each time you throw the hoop over the stick, you could have, let's say, five moments of joy each time you play. And it wouldn't even matter if you won.'

"'More than that grandpa,' I remember telling him," Ma Ma Gombe said, and smiled as she recalled that moment. "'I almost always get seven or more when I play.'"

"'Well then you would get seven moments of joy even if you didn't win, and eight moments of joy if you did win,' he told me.

"'But it's not the same,' I protested. 'The feeling isn't the same.'

"'Well who decides that?' he asked."

Ma Ma Gombe smiled again. "And with that little question, he changed the world for me. I started celebrating every throw of the ring, and double celebrating every throw that went over the stick, and triple celebrating every time I won. And I won even more games too. From that point on, I was the happiest hoop player that has probably ever lived."

And from that point on in Ma Ma Gombe's and my journey, I stopped focusing on how far we were going to walk each day, and began celebrating every step that we took.

# 8

One late afternoon during our third week of traveling, I noticed that the terrain ahead looked different. The flat plains were giving way to small, rolling hills and forests. We camped that night on the edge of the tree line.

As we were preparing to sleep, Ma Ma Gombe said to me, "Tomorrow I will show you Adoo, young Jack. Tomorrow you will see your first elephant."

She was correct. The next day I did see my first elephant. And I almost died in the process.

The morning started out fine. We woke with the sun and followed a trail into the thicket of trees. As we walked, Ma Ma Gombe motioned for me to be quiet, and to walk slowly and carefully. Above our heads, I could see families of monkeys jumping from branch to branch. Occasionally a battle would break out between two of them, and the jungle would come alive with the shrieking and howling of the combatants.

We exited the jungle into a large clearing and Ma Ma

Gombe motioned for me to stop. Directly in front of us was a large pool of muddy water surrounded by reddish dirt and sand. The jungle behind us was giving way to more open, rolling hills, and the pool of water sat on a small plain between the two.

Ma Ma Gombe sat down. "They will arrive soon," she said and motioned for me to sit.

I had barely positioned myself on the ground when I saw them. There were two groups, one coming from the trees we had just left, and another group coming down from the hills beyond the water. The group coming from the trees had eight elephants of different sizes.

"That is one family," Ma Ma Gombe said. "Elephant families are ruled by a matriarch. That one there is the leader."

I looked to where Ma Ma Gombe was pointing. There was a large female elephant at the front of the group.

"She will take care of the family until she passes on, and then one of her oldest female offspring will take over. Someday perhaps that little one will be in charge."

Ma Ma Gombe motioned toward a little baby elephant no bigger than four feet tall, who was running amongst the larger ones.

"How long do they live?" I asked.

"More than seventy years, young Jack," she replied. "If left alone."

As the two groups converged on the water hole, they began to trumpet, and bump against one another.

"Is it dangerous?" I asked.

"No," she said, smiling and never taking her eyes off of them. "They are just two families greeting each other. It is their way of saying hello."

One by one, the elephants began to immerse themselves in the pool. They would fill their trunks with water, and splash it over their heads. As we sat watching, more elephants began to appear from both the jungle and the hills. By mid-morning, Ma Ma Gombe and I were sitting no more than a stone's throw from over sixty elephants.

My concentration on them was interrupted by a rustling sound from behind us. I was about to turn, when Ma Ma Gombe put her hand on my shoulder.

"Slowly, young Jack. Always move slowly around the elephants. Besides, it is just my friend, Kimasa."

I slowly turned and as I did, a young man of about sixteen dropped down beside Ma Ma Gombe.

"Hello, Ma Ma Gombe," he said, with a wide, bright smile.

"Hello, Kimasa," she replied, and hugged his head to hers. "Kimasa, this is my friend, Jack. He has never seen elephants before."

As Kimasa turned to me, his smile faded.

"Poachers," he said.

I turned and followed his gaze to the edge of the tree line. Two men with guns were slowly sneaking up to within shooting distance of the elephants. Kimasa whistled a sharp blast from between his teeth. Immediately, someone from the trees returned the whistle, and then three more whistles followed in close unison. The men with the guns paused and looked around, trying to locate the sound of the whistles.

The sounds had also alerted the elephants. A group of seven large males began to trumpet and weave their heads back and forth. They quickly spotted the poachers, who were more out in the open than we were, and formed a wall between them and the females and calves.

I looked over at the poachers. They were a good hundred yards from the tree line now, and seemed to be evaluating their options of running or still shooting one of the elephants. In that moment, one of the bull elephants charged them.

When that happened, two men emerged from the jungle and began to whistle, as Kimasa had. And then the poachers began to run—right toward *us*.

# 9

Kimasa turned to me. "We have to stop them. If they get away, they will come back and kill the elephants."

"And if they see us, they might shoot us," I replied.

"Then don't let them see you," he said.

I turned to ask Ma Ma Gombe what to do, but she was gone. I turned back to face Kimasa, and he was gone.

The men were now less than fifty yards away. I was crouching low in the grass next to the tree where we had been sitting, so they couldn't see me. But I knew that in the next few moments they would be right on top of me. The shorter man was considerably faster than the other, and he was running ahead of his companion by about forty feet.

Just as he was about to run me over, Ma Ma Gombe leapt up from a spot where she had hidden in the grass, and began yelling at him. He stopped running, and shouldered his gun to shoot her.

In a rush of instinct, I threw my body at his. He hadn't seen

me, and the surprise knocked him over and his gun flew into the grass. As I scrambled to my feet, I heard a crack and felt a sharp pain. I looked up and saw the other poacher cocking his rifle for a second shot.

He never got the chance. Kimasa had been waiting for him, and as the poacher aimed his rifle, Kimasa knocked him to his feet.

Within moments, Kimasa's friends were upon the two poachers, and the fight was over.

That night, Kimasa, Ma Ma Gombe, and I sat together by the campfire. Ma Ma Gombe had gone into the forest and returned with some leaves, which she mashed together in a small clay bowl.

"This will help ease the pain," she said, as she applied the mixture to my arm where the bullet had grazed it. "You are very lucky. A few inches toward your chest, and neither this nor anything else would have done you much good."

It had taken me almost an hour after the incident to stop shaking. I had never come that close to dying before.

"You were very brave, young Jack," Ma Ma Gombe said. "You saved my life today."

"I thought he was going to shoot you," I said.

"Yes, I know," she replied. "And he would have if you had not stopped him."

"Why were they out there?" I asked.

"They are poachers," replied Kimasa. "They kill the elephants and then leave them to rot after they take their tusks. Why do they do it?" he asked Ma Ma Gombe. "Why do they want the tusks? They are just like bones."

Ma Ma Gombe sat silently.

"I know," I said quietly. "They sell them."

"For what?" he asked.

"People carve them, and then they sell it as artwork."

"But why don't they carve wood, or stone?"

Ma Ma Gombe turned to him, "Because people will pay much money for carvings from the tusks," she replied sadly.

He looked at us in amazement. "But do the people not realize that an elephant must die for each of those carvings? Even the largest tusks cannot weigh more than one hundred pounds. They believe in killing a giant elephant who would live for seventy years, and who is a member of a family, for two hundred pounds of something to carve?"

"Yes," Ma Ma Gombe replied. "I know it sounds foolish, but yes."

Kimasa shook his head, "I do not believe that if those people saw what a beautiful piece of artwork each elephant is while alive, they would ever again justify killing it for a piece of its tusk. How can that be part of their Big Five for Life, Ma Ma Gombe?"

She shook her head and said softly, "I am sure it is not, Kimasa. I am sure it is not."

# 10

The next morning when I woke, Kimasa and his friends had already gone. They had taken the poachers with them. Ma Ma Gombe and I returned to our tree near the water hole, and for the next two days we watched the elephants. It was marvelous. They are such giant creatures, and yet so playful and friendly. The mothers care for their babies, the young adolescents romp and play with each other. It is not so different than watching humans at a swimming pool.

"Ma Ma Gombe, do you believe elephants have a Big Five for Life?"

"Yes, I do," she replied. "I believe they want to be an elephant, not a carving in some person's home. I believe they want to wander and see the world. I believe they want to raise their children. I believe they want to love.

"I believe all creatures have a Big Five for Life, young Jack. We humans are just the ones who seem most disconnected from ours."

I nodded, "Ma Ma Gombe, regarding the other day—I didn't envision fulfilling my Big Five for Life would be so dangerous."

"Sometimes life is not an easy path," she replied. "But that does not mean we should stop moving. We grow stronger with each step forward, and we grow weaker when we make no progress at all."

"Before you took this trip," she asked, "what were you afraid of?"

"I don't know," I replied.

"Yes you do," she said, and looked into my eyes. "What were you afraid of?"

I glanced down at the ground, "I guess I was afraid of little things, like approaching someone I didn't know, or trying something I didn't know how to do."

"Think of what happened here," she said. "After what you did two days ago, I do not think approaching someone you don't know will still make you afraid.

"When we move forward, it makes us stronger. It takes away our fear. Eventually there comes a day when we have progressed so far, that we do not even fear death."

She looked at me again. "If you had died because of the poachers, you would have died in the pursuit of your Big Five for Life, young Jack. People die every day never having gotten

that far. They die a slow painful death wondering what their life might be like if only they could find the courage to pursue it. And for most of them, their Big Five for Life is far less dangerous than hiking through Africa to see elephants.

# 11

One morning we crossed over a small rise of hills, and as I looked out in the distance I could see a village.

"Kamatubu," Ma Ma Gombe said. "We will stay there for the next few days."

It had been weeks since we last saw any people, and I was amazed at how unusual it felt to be around so many of them.

As we walked up the dusty street, cries erupted when the people recognized Ma Ma Gombe. People ran from their doors to yell greetings, and when the word reached the school that "Ma Ma Gombe is here," the students came streaming out to greet her, like ants leaving their mound.

Within minutes she was surrounded by children. They were dancing, and singing, and yelling "Ma Ma Gombe, Ma Ma Gombe." Finally, after many minutes, Ma Ma Gombe was able to calm them down enough so that they could hear her.

"You are like a bunch of unruly meerkats," she said smiling and hugging the children. "How are my little Big Five for

Life adventurers?"

Then the air was alive again, as each child tried to explain how they had progressed on their Big Five for Life since last seeing Ma Ma Gombe.

"Easy little ones, easy," she said, smiling the entire time.

By now their teacher had come forth and Ma Ma Gombe spotted her watching and smiling at the children's enthusiasm.

"And there is your beautiful teacher. I have missed you, Arika," Ma Ma Gombe said, and hugged the teacher.

"I have missed you too, Ma Ma Gombe. We all have."

Beautiful did not begin to describe Arika. She had deep brown skin, bright eyes, and a majestic forehead that reminded me of the Nubian queens I had read about in my history books. Her high cheek bones were accented by small white dots applied in geometric patterns on her skin. They made her look alluring and mysterious.

Some of the children noticed that I could not take my eyes from her, and they began to giggle.

"And this is my friend," Ma Ma Gombe said. "His name is Jack, and he is pursuing his Big Five for Life."

"I think he's in love with Ms. Arika," said one of the smaller girls, which brought peals of laughter from the children and shades of red to my cheeks.

"Enough, enough, enough," Ma Ma Gombe replied laugh-

ingly. "We are interrupting your school time. Why don't we meet later today at the big tree," she said and pointed to a massive shade tree at the top of one of the smaller hills outside of town.

"When you are done with school, come find us there. We want to hear all about your latest adventures."

# 12

The discussions I watched take place that afternoon, were one of the highlights of my African experience. I had never witnessed children so enthused about their existence. When we gathered under the giant tree, Ma Ma Gombe asked each child to stand in front of the group and explain what their Big Five for Life were, and why they had chosen them.

Then the children shared what they had done to achieve their Big Five for Life since they had last seen Ma Ma Gombe. It was magical. Each and every child was thriving on their existence. As each took their turn, they would finish by asking if Ma Ma Gombe or I, or anyone else could help them. It seemed that Ma Ma Gombe had an answer for each child.

For the little girl who wanted to see a monkey, Ma Ma Gombe told her about a forest three days away, where we had seen hundreds of little red spider monkeys. Two of the older children offered to take her there.

An older boy of about fourteen, named Bonabu, wanted to

know how to bring more water to the earth, so that his father's plants would grow taller and produce more. Ma Ma Gombe shared with him how we had passed farmers in a much drier region who were digging deep furrows and putting the plants inside them. That way the shade from the furrow would keep the sun off of them longer, the wind would not blow them over, and the rain would collect more efficiently.

When it was her turn, one of the older girls explained that seeing the ocean was part of her Big Five for Life. Ma Ma Gombe smiled at her. "That was one of my first Big Five for Life too, Gilana. It is one of the magical moments of life, to look out upon the ocean and see water for as far as your eyes can look.

"And there are dolphin, which are similar to giant fish, but which actually breathe air just like you and me. They come in close to shore to feed, and if you sit in the water and spin around and make squeaking noises, they will come right up to you."

Ma Ma Gombe explained how the waves seemed endless in the way they crashed against the shore, only to recede back out into the surf and form the basis for the next wave. She also told Gilana how she could swim with penguins if she went to one particular beach along the African coast.

"There are so many you cannot count them," Ma Ma Gombe explained. "They are like little black and white birds, except they live in the water and on the land, and they all walk like this."

With that, she waddled back and forth like a penguin, to the shrieks of laughter from the children.

"But when they get to the water, they throw themselves in and swim faster than an arrow," she said. "And you can swim with them."

I looked at Gilana. She was beaming. She could see it all in her head—the ocean, the waves, the penguins, the dolphin. Ma Ma Gombe was enabling her to see her dream.

As if sensing my thoughts, Ma Ma Gombe said to the children, "Remember my little ones, every Big Five for Life begins with a dream. And a dream is simply a reality waiting to happen."

Ma Ma Gombe turned to Gilana, "Did you make that necklace you're wearing?"

Around Gilana's neck was a beautiful necklace of bluish green stones intermixed with others that had a red marbled hue and still others that were solid black.

"Yes, Ma Ma Gombe," Gilana replied.

Ma Ma Gombe nodded. "If you want to go to the ocean, then make many of those necklaces. Make as many as you can carry, and when the Wantari bring their cattle through here next year, ask the women if you can go along with them.

"They will only go about half-way from here to the ocean, but at the place where they stop and sell their cattle is a beau-

tiful little town. Go to the store there and tell the owner Ma Ma Gombe sent you. He will buy your necklaces and if you explain to him that you want to see the ocean, he will help you get the rest of the way.

"He is an old friend of mine, and he used to spend his life upon great ships that sailed the oceans. He will understand why what you seek is so important to you."

# 13

After the last of the children had gone, Ma Ma Gombe, Arika, and I sat beneath the tree.

"I have never seen children so full of life," I said. "They have less here than most of the children where I live, but they seem to love life so much more. They have far more enthusiasm, they ask for help, they help each other, they are fearless, and they are so focused…"

"That is all the work of Arika," Ma Ma Gombe replied. "She is the one who has been teaching them the Big Five for Life."

I looked at Arika. It was hard not to look at her. Her glow, which had appeared strong when we walked into the village, was now radiant.

"I am simply fulfilling part of my Big Five for Life, and passing along what a wise, wise woman once taught me when I was a very little girl," Arika said and hugged Ma Ma Gombe. "It is very gratifying to hear you say that though, Jack."

"And this is how it works," Ma Ma Gombe commented.

"As you have taught them Arika, so eventually will Gilana be a teacher to those who wish to see the ocean. And Bonabu will teach the farmers in the next village once he masters how to furrow his crops.

"With each success, the power of the Big Five for Life grows. With each success, there are more Who's in the world, helping people do, see, and experience what they want in their lives."

"Who's?" I asked.

Ma Ma Gombe stood up and brushed the grass from her cape. "I am afraid that today's activities have left me a bit tired, my two young friends," she said. "Arika, perhaps you can share with Jack what you teach the children about Who's. It would be valuable for him in his journey, and he has not yet heard it from me."

Arika stood up, "Ma Ma Gombe, let me take you to my home. You can take a nap and then stay with me. I have plenty of room. And you as well, Jack. I have another room that you can use."

"No, you two stay here," Ma Ma Gombe replied. "You have much to talk about. I will go to your place, Arika, and the two of you can meet me there later."

I watched Ma Ma Gombe walk down the hill. Then I turned toward Arika. I wanted to memorize every curve on her face, so I would never forget it. I looked in her eyes and she smiled.

"Ma Ma Gombe is quite a Who, isn't she?" she asked.

"I'm not sure what that means, but I've been traveling with her for over two months now, and I don't think I've ever seen her get tired."

"I think she just wanted us to be alone," Arika said and smiled again. "She's a romantic at heart."

I felt my cheeks start to turn a little red. "And apparently also a Who," I replied, "Although I don't know what that means."

"A Who is someone who helps you avoid Mad How disease, Jack," Arika replied, as her eyes danced with playfulness.

"Well, that certainly clears everything up."

She laughed. "When people figure out their Big Five for Life, they are in a unique situation. They know where their life is at, and they also know where they want their life to go. So what question do they need to ask?"

"Well, if they know where they are, and they know where they want to get to, I guess they ask 'How do I get there?'" I replied.

"Ah, and then they would be yet another victim of Mad How disease," Arika replied.

I laughed, "That's Mad How disease?"

"Yes, were you expecting something different?"

"Well, given some of the things I had to get shots for before coming here to Africa, that doesn't sound so bad."

"You underestimate the debilitating impact of Mad How disease," she said and smiled. "It is worse than Malaria, Dengue, Yellow Fever, and all the rest of them combined.

"You see, when someone asks 'How do I get there?' they encounter things like barriers, learning curves, and obstacles. I teach my students that each encounter is like a mountain. When someone hits the first mountain they are full of energy and passion for their Big Five for Life.

"They spend days, weeks, and sometimes even years figuring out how to get over it. Eventually their energy and passion enables them to find the answer and get over the mountain. Unfortunately, just beyond that is a second mountain, and although they make it over that one too, their energy and passion and time are drained even further.

"By the time they hit the third mountain, they have no energy, no passion, and no time left. So they give up. They are a victim of Mad How disease. Their Big Five for Life remains just over the horizon and unfulfilled for their entire existence.

"And because they don't do, see, or experience the five things that they have determined would make their life a success—they die a failure in their own eyes.

"And that is why it's worse than Malaria, Dengue, Yellow Fever and all the rest of them combined. Because there is nothing more tragic than a life that does not meet the expectations

of the person who is living it."

"I see," I said slowly, while letting her words sink in. "So then how does someone avoid Mad How disease?"

"That's where the Who comes in. Instead of asking 'How do I get from where I am to where I want to go?' the person asks 'Who has already gotten from where I am to where I want to go?' Then they find out what the Who did, and they imitate it.

"You see, with rare exception, no matter what is on your Big Five for Life list, some person, at some point, at some place in the history of the world, has done, seen, or experienced what you want to do, see or experience. And if you imitate their actions, you will fly over the mountains, not have to climb them."

"What happens if you find out what they did, and you don't like the way they did it?" I asked.

"Then you find another Who."

"And if you actually do pick something that no one has ever done, seen, or experienced before?"

"Then find a Who who has done, seen, or experienced something close, and see what parts of that you can imitate."

"We have an expression where I live," I said. "'Don't recreate the wheel.' The person who said that must have been familiar with something similar to finding your Who."

I looked at Arika, "Who are your Who's?"

She smiled, "I have many. Ma Ma Gombe is a very signifi-

cant one. My sister is seven years older than me, and for many things she is one. Perhaps you are one as well, Jack," she said and smiled again.

# 14

Over the next four days, Arika and I had many talks. It turned out that I *was* a Who for her on some things, and she was a Who for my goal of learning about Africa. She had studied to be a naturalist, a passion fueled by Ma Ma Gombe. During our walks each day, she helped me understand how everything in Africa, and really everything in the world, is connected.

Since I had only figured out one of my Big Five for Life, it was impossible for her to assist me with any others. We talked about that one evening.

"In the same way that there is an energy that is constantly flowing through us, and the trees, and the mountains, and the animals, I believe that our Who's are always present," she explained.

"It is not that when the student is ready the teacher appears, as the philosophy books say. It is that the teacher is always there, it just depends on whether the student knows what type of teacher they are looking for. Ma Ma Gombe shared a story with

me when I was a child that I have always remembered.

"'Imagine,' she said, 'if no one ever told the lioness that she was a hunter. There would be tracks on the ground, but she would not see them. The wind would bring scents to her nose, but she would not smell them. The air would fill with the sounds from herds of animals, but she would not hear them.'

"Our Who's can be all around us, but we have to know our Big Five for Life before we can recognize that the Who's are there."

# 15

Five days after our arrival, Ma Ma Gombe and I bid farewell to the people of the village. During our stay, Ma Ma Gombe had made a point of spending much individual time with Arika and each of the children. It was only later that I would better understand why she did that.

There was one girl in particular that Ma Ma Gombe spent the most time with. When Arika and I would go for our walks, Ma Ma Gombe would almost always visit her. When we were leaving, she stood and held Ma Ma Gombe for a long time. The constant stream of tears down her cheeks indicated that much had passed between them.

After we left the village behind, Ma Ma Gombe explained that the girl had gotten married very young, and that her husband was now beating her almost every day.

"She used to have such passion for life," Ma Ma Gombe explained. "Now she just wishes it would be over and done with."

"And you understand what she is going through?" I asked.

"I have *lived* what she is going through," Ma Ma Gombe responded quietly.

Ma Ma Gombe remained silent for many hours after that. We walked up mountain paths among fir trees and giant granite outcroppings. When we reached the top of one of the lower peaks, Ma Ma Gombe gazed back at the land below.

"This is a beautiful playground we have been given," she said. "Sometimes it is difficult to remember that."

"What do you mean?" I asked.

"When I was a young girl, I knew very little of the world. My parents were very poor, and although I was smart, I did not have much of an education. I fell in love with a man from a neighboring village. I knew almost nothing about him, but I thought that I loved him, and I thought that love would conquer all.

"He turned out to be one of my greatest teachers," she said.

"In what way?"

"Within weeks of our marriage, he began to belittle me. He would insult me in front of others, and call me stupid because I didn't know things. Things that he didn't know either, as it would turn out. But at the time I didn't realize that. The more I begged for his love, the worse he became.

"Then he began to beat me. I felt afraid. I felt ashamed. We lived in his village and I knew almost no one, and the ones I did know did nothing to help me. They too were some of my great-

est teachers.

"When I was four months pregnant with my first baby, he beat me so violently that I lost the child. Up until that point I had become gradually more and more numb to my reality. But that was more than I could take. My mother had not received much education, but she had been a loving parent. I had yearned for the chance to be one too, to hold my child in my arms, rock it to sleep, and teach it about life. But he took that away.

"There was always a period between the beatings during which he would let me heal. In the past, I had taken those to be signs that he was changing, that everything would be fine, that he would love me. This time I was not so foolish. I continued to pretend that my injuries were bad, until I had fully healed.

"Then one morning when he was off on a hunt, I walked away. And on that morning I began my life again."

"I'm sorry, Ma Ma Gombe," I said quietly. I didn't know how else to respond. "Do you still hate him?" I asked.

"No," she replied and shook her head. "I learned a great deal about life because of him."

She spread her arms wide and looked out at the valley stretched below us, and at the shimmering lake nestled between the lower hills. "And I learned a great deal about how all of this works.

"I believe that we are something before we are born, young

Jack, and I believe that we are something after we die. Do you believe that?"

"Yes, I do," I replied. "Although I don't know why I believe it."

"Well, when you believe that you were something before, and will be something after, it leaves an interesting question," Ma Ma Gombe said. "And that is, 'Why are you here?' Why do we visit this beautiful place if we are just coming from somewhere on the way to somewhere else?

"I believe the answer is that this place is like a school," she said. "And before we arrive, we pick certain things that we would like to learn while we are here, certain challenges we would like to try to overcome during our life.

"I think of it like one of those giant signs down by the docks, where they list all the boats that are leaving and the places they are going. Only instead of picking boats, we pick challenges.

"I'll take fear of failure please," she said, and pointed up at the sky, as if she were choosing her challenges from some giant board. "And how about a lack of self confidence, and an oppressive person in my life perhaps...

"We select these challenges so that our experience here in the playground means more to us," she continued. "Imagine trying to kick a ball into a goal if no one was playing defense or guarding the goal. For the first few times it would be exciting, but soon it would be boring. No, young Jack, the excitement

comes when we have learned to evade the defender, and when we shoot past the goal keeper."

Ma Ma Gombe paused, and looked out on the horizon again. "And so we pick the challenges that when we have learned to go beyond them, then we will have truly learned something. We will have truly accomplished something.

"And we don't know exactly how the challenges are going to manifest themselves," she said. "We just know we will face them during our time in the playground.

"But then we are born, and we don't remember what we picked. We don't remember that we came from somewhere else, and are going somewhere after this. We just see the game, and we see the defenders, and we wish it were easier.

"And at an almost non-stop pace, the universe tries to remind us of those challenges that *we* picked. The universe is trying to inspire us to win the game, to rise above the level of the defenders.

"The reminders start off small and almost painless. But when we don't take heed of them, the universe increases the intensity of the reminder. What was once a gentle tap on the shoulder becomes thunder and lightning, and then a rain storm of reminders, until we either remember, or eventually we die.

"And for those who do remember, and take on the challenges, and overcome them—which we always can, or we wouldn't have

picked them to begin with—the sky parts, and the world looks like this," she said, and indicated the view in front of us.

"We see the paradise that the playground really is."

She paused for a moment. "When my husband beat me so much that I lost my baby, it was my rainstorm. It was my wake up call to remember where I came from, why I am here, and where I go after this.

"We choose our challenges, young Jack. I was trying to help that young girl remember how she chose hers—before the universe brings the type of reminder I went through."

I looked at Ma Ma Gombe. "How is it that you don't still hate him, after what he did to you? I hate him and I never even met him. And I hate the man who is doing that to her."

"One of my Big Five for Life is to meet people from all around the world," she replied. "I had wanted to do that ever since I read one particular book when I was very young. It was a story about children from countries much different than mine, and it fascinated me.

"I had put that dream away when my husband began to beat me. But when I left the village that morning, I made the decision to make that dream a reality. I didn't know how I was going to do it, but I knew it was what I wanted.

"After three days of walking, I came upon a camp of travelers. Their cook had abandoned them, and had taken most of their

food supplies. Their guide asked me if I could help. I went out that afternoon and gathered roots and herbs and cooked them with what their guide had killed. And with that I was on my way to fulfilling my dream.

"One of the women in the group was a playwright, and it was something I learned from her that enabled me to not hate him.

"I had never heard of a play before. She explained to me that it was people pretending to be different things. They acted a certain way so that the audience would have a particular experience. Each actor had certain roles to play, and lines to read, and actions to take, to make their role believable.

"One night I was lying out, looking up at the stars, and it suddenly all became very clear to me. I came here to experience life. I made it more difficult for myself by picking certain challenges to overcome. And in choosing that, someone had to play the part of the defender. Someone had to read certain lines, and act a certain way to make the challenges seem believable.

"And I had a vision that when I would die, I would not just see all the people who had been my friends, and supporters during my life, but I would realize that all the people who had represented my biggest challenges, were in fact, just actors in my play.

"That under their breath as they were reading their lines, they were saying 'Break free, Gombe. Don't listen to me. These

are just lines from a play. Break free.' And I would see all of those people too, and they would be cheering the loudest. For they were the ones most hopeful that I would see beyond their costumes and their lines.

"Their greatest wish was that I would overcome them, and fulfill my Big Five for Life.

"That is why I do not hate him, young Jack. I see him for what he was and for what role he played in my life."

I sat in silence for a few minutes. "Are you saying that what he did to you was ok?"

"Young Jack, there is a difference between knowing people are actors in our lives and continuing to let them play a particular role. When you understand it is a play, you also understand that you are directing the play. For me it is not about ok, or not ok. It is about empowering myself to choose what my play is going to be like, and who I allow to be in it."

# 16

On an overcast morning where the fog was so dense I could barely see five feet in front of me, Ma Ma Gombe told me I was about to see my first rhinoceros.

"I don't think we can see anything, Ma Ma Gombe. This fog is so thick I can barely see you, and you are just a few feet away."

"It will break when the sun comes out," Ma Ma Gombe replied. "Now hurry, we must go to where they are while the fog is still here."

Ma Ma Gombe guided me down the small hill where we had camped for the night. We walked through what seemed like the end of time. Everywhere I looked, all I could see were vague shapes of trees, boulders, and many things that in the fog appeared unrecognizable. I had no idea where we were going, and I made sure that Ma Ma Gombe did not get far ahead of me. The thought of being out in the middle of the fog alone, was not a pleasant one.

After an hour, Ma Ma Gombe indicated I should walk

as quietly as possible, and we shouldn't talk. The fog had not cleared, but even with the low visibility I could see we were walking among short scrub trees that were about six feet tall. They had tiny little leaves and spindly branches reaching out in all directions.

It was difficult to not step on the dead branches that had fallen into the path. Each time I accidentally stepped on one it would generate a loud cracking noise from beneath my feet, and a look of concern from Ma Ma Gombe.

Then, all of a sudden, there appeared in front of us a small rise, no higher than four or five feet. It was a giant rock, that as we got closer, I could see had broken off from a tall stone cliff directly behind it. Ma Ma Gombe climbed up on the rock and sat down. I followed, and as I eased down next to her, she put her hand close to my ear.

"Enjoy each moment of this morning, young Jack," she whispered. "The world is about to unfold in front of you."

And unfold it did. As the sun rose into the sky, the images in front of me changed by the second. At first it was the way everything looked through the fog. Each branch of the trees, and each tall blade of the waist-high elephant grass took on an iridescent glow as the drops of moisture from the fog reflected the few rays of light that were able to penetrate through the dense air.

Then it was the sounds. The complete quiet of the fog filled

early morning gave way to the flutter of wings, and the calls of birds, as they began to fly from their nests in the cliffs above us. I could hear the hum of insects become increasingly louder, and the cracking of branches as animals began to move in the underbrush around us.

And then it was the sky. As the fog began to disappear, the white feathery clouds on the horizon turned from gray, to pink, and then to bright orange as the sun began its ascent into the sky. And with its ascent, the whole world came alive.

At that moment I felt as though I was in the presence of God. I felt as if this was exactly what our world had been created for. It was beyond beautiful, it was stunning.

Ma Ma Gombe touched my shoulder and pointed. Not twenty yards away, was a single, large tree rising up among the small scrub foliage. The fog had been so thick when we arrived, that I hadn't seen it. On one of the large overhanging branches, a full grown leopard rose to its feet, arched its back, and stretched, digging its claws deep into the tree branch.

Then, like a practiced tight-rope walker, it leisurely turned on the branch, walked to the trunk, and descended face first onto the ground below.

My body went tight and I looked at Ma Ma Gombe, but she slowly shook her head back and forth, indicating not to worry. The leopard walked to a pool of water at the base of the cliff, and

I watched it lap its tongue in the clear pond. It stretched again, raising its hind quarters high up in the air and tucking its head forward. Then it disappeared into the grass.

I watched where it had gone for a few moments until Ma Ma Gombe touched my shoulder again. I turned and followed her gaze. There were four full-grown rhinoceros grazing not fifty feet from us. Ma Ma Gombe very slowly put her hand to my ear and whispered.

"Make very small and slow motions if you have to move. Rhinoceros have very poor eyesight, but they will attack movement or sounds if they are surprised or become angry."

Each of the animals stood over six feet tall, and were more than twelve feet long. Their horns were like giant curved thorns rising four feet from their snouts.

"What amazing looking creatures," I thought to myself. Their gray skin looked like thick layers of pliable armor, and their presence brought to mind an impenetrable object. It seemed an odd paradox to watch these massive, muscular animals chewing on leaves and grass.

If there was ever an animal designed to intimidate predators from attacking, this was it.

We watched the rhinoceros all morning. After the fog had completely lifted, I was able to see that we were seated on a rock platform at the base of a curving cliff. The small pond next to

us was generated from rain water that cascaded down from the cliffs above. It was the perfect place from which to watch the animals.

Along with the rhinoceros and the leopard, we saw many other animals that morning including bushbuck, eland, kudu, and tiny little Thompson gazelles. A whole family of warthogs began to walk right up onto our rock ledge until they realized we were there, and then scampered off. And as we were leaving, a mother elephant walked through the trees in front of us with her little one right behind her.

It was perfection. I had dreamed of seeing these animals for so long, and had imagined what it would be like. What I had not been able to imagine was the energy and physical sensations that would accompany the experience. Feeling the soft morning breeze on my arms, the warmth from the sun on my face, the tremble of the earth whenever the rhinoceros would become agitated and stamp their feet…

It was one thing to imagine it. It was so much more to experience it. I was living my Big Five for Life.

# 17

"You are very quiet this morning, young Jack," Ma Ma Gombe said to me a few days after we had seen the rhinoceros.

"I've been thinking," I replied. "I'm trying to figure out what I'm going to do when I go back to reality. I've enjoyed my months here more than the rest of my life put together. I don't know how I can go back."

We were walking through a grove of palms and thick brush. Ma Ma Gombe turned to me. "Young Jack, put your hand around this tree."

I turned to look at the tree she was motioning toward. It was a type of palm I'd never seen before I came to Africa. The entire length of the trunk was covered in 4-inch long spikes.

Ma Ma Gombe saw me hesitating. "Put your hand around this palm tree, young Jack. No, on second thought, hug the tree. Hug it as hard as you can."

I reached my hand out and touched the spikes. They were solid.

"Ma Ma Gombe, I can't hug this tree. There must be a thousand spines on there. If I hug this, my whole body is going to be speared."

"That cannot be," she replied and again indicated that I should hug the tree.

I reached for the spines on a different section. They too were solid and sharp.

"Ma Ma Gombe, the whole tree is covered in spines. I can't hug it."

"You just told me that you were contemplating what you would do when you went back to reality," Ma Ma Gombe replied. "If this is not reality, then you should be able to hug the tree. If this is not reality, then there are no spines to poke you."

I looked at her confused.

"Be very careful, young Jack. Our words can tell our mind what to believe. And if we say the same words long enough, even our soul begins to think they are real.

"Are these trees not real?" she asked. "Were not the rhinoceros and the leopard we saw a few days ago real? Am I not real?

"When you say that something else is real, and this is not, you are saying to your soul that you cannot have this, that you do not deserve to have this.

"Too many people believe that what they spend their time at is more real than what they would like to spend their time at."

"But this isn't my reality, Ma Ma Gombe," I protested.

"Do you want me to ask you to hug the tree again?" she asked.

"No," I replied.

"This *is* your reality, young Jack. Right now, right here, everything is real. This is your reality. If you were to never go back, would the other type of life you lived still exist?"

"Yes," I replied. "Not for me, but for whoever was living it."

"And would you not be living here in a very real world while that other type of life still existed?" she asked.

"Yes."

Ma Ma Gombe laughed.

"What is it?" I asked.

"At the same time you are claiming this cannot be your reality because it isn't real, there is probably an old woman somewhere in a place like where you used to live having this same exact discussion with a young African man.

"Only he is claiming that your old type of life can't be his reality because this is real and that isn't. Meanwhile you are here with me claiming that this—his old reality—can't be real because what he is doing is real.

She shook her head, "Young Jack, the way we live our life, the way we exist, our environment, what we do every day, all of it is what we choose it to be. Anything can be our reality—

the minute we open our minds and realize it is just as real and just as much of an option as any other."

# 18

In addition to the animals, part of what made my experience with Ma Ma Gombe so fascinating was the people she introduced me to.

One afternoon as we rested in the shade of a large tree, a goat herder appeared on the far side of the grass-filled valley we were in. As he approached, I could see that he was an older man, although not quite as old as Ma Ma Gombe.

He came upon the tree where we were, and sat down as his goats grazed in the open grass.

"Ma Ma Gombe, I see you have a new adventurer with you," he said.

"Yes," she replied. "This is Jack. He is here to fulfill part of his Big Five for Life."

"Ah, you are so lucky," he said to her. "Always wandering the countryside, meeting new people. I wish my life was more like yours, Ma Ma Gombe. I am always worrying about the lions trying to steal my goats, or some of my animals wandering off.

And there is no one to talk to every day."

I introduced myself to the man and commented, "If goat herding isn't to your liking, why not do something else?"

"I am Epelpo," he replied back. "And what would I do? I am a goat herder."

"Is that part of your Big Five for Life?" I asked.

"Ah, he truly is one of your adventurers, Ma Ma Gombe," he said and laughed. "Another one who talks of the Big Five for Life." He turned to face me. "I don't even know what my Big Five for Life are. And if I did know them, how would I do them? I have my goats to manage."

"Maybe you could sell the goats," I replied.

"Sell my goats? I have worked my whole life to have a herd this large. Besides, this is the only thing I know how to do well."

"Maybe you could learn to do something else," I replied. "How long did it take you to learn about herding goats?"

"One never stops learning about goats," he replied. "There is always more to do. If I just had my freedom like you and Ma Ma Gombe, maybe then I would have time to think about my Big Five for Life. It is easy for you. Each year my herd gets bigger and bigger though. It is not so easy for me."

Our conversation went on in a very similar fashion for a few more minutes. Ma Ma Gombe said nothing, and eventually I stopped talking too. Soon Epelpo got to his feet.

"I must keep moving," he said. "There are many things to do. I wish I could sit here and admire the scenery and think about my Big Five for Life, like the two of you, but someone must take care of the goats."

When he had gone I turned to Ma Ma Gombe. "You were awfully quiet during that conversation."

She smiled, "I thought you should experience Epelpo in your own way."

"He could do so much," I said. "Why doesn't he sell half of his herd and leave himself with half the responsibility, or pay someone else to watch the herd every once in a while? He is so busy clinging to his unhappiness he can't see that he's got it backwards.

"He said that when he gets more freedom, *then* he will think about his Big Five for Life, and when he's happier, *then* he will think about his Big Five for Life.

"He doesn't see that if he was fulfilling his Big Five for Life, then he would *have* freedom, and he would *be* happy. What he *should* do is…"

"No, young Jack," Ma Ma Gombe interrupted. "Be careful with your words. If we do not want to be told what we should be doing with our life, then we must not do that to others. It is his life. And those challenges you saw are his to overcome."

"It just seems like there are so many options for what he

could do," I said.

"Yes, there are. But he must decide them, not you or I. If you had talked more, Epelpo would have told you that he does what he does for his family. He has told me many times that his wife and children depend on him and that is why he cannot change.

"When Epelpo started, he had five goats. Over time he grew that to twenty goats, and now to his current herd, which is many many goats. Yet always he has been worried that it is not enough."

"How many children does he have?" I asked.

"Five," she replied. "They do not know their father very well. He has spent most of his life looking for better pastures, where the goats would get fat and have good babies. That way he would have plenty of goats for his family. So now his children are all almost grown. They have had very little interaction with their father, and few memories of anything except him coming and going. But they have many goats. And such is his choice."

# 19

We were still sitting beneath the tree and I was thinking about Epelpo's comments.

"Did you ever have another child, Ma Ma Gombe? After you left your husband when he beat you?"

"Yes," she said and smiled. "I had two. A boy and a girl."

"Where are they now?" I asked.

She paused and looked out on the horizon. "Africa has taken them back," she replied.

"Oh, I'm sorry."

"Do not be sorry, young Jack. You had nothing to do with it, and they lived extraordinary lives. They each fulfilled their Big Five for Life, and in the process lived lives that most people only dream of."

"Was it hard to let them go?" I asked.

"They are your babies," she replied. "It is always hard to let them go. When they are alive you want to keep them from danger. When they are gone, you know they are simply done with

this part of their journey, but still you miss them. It is always hard to let them go.

"But each arrives with their own challenges to overcome. To try to shield them from the very challenges they chose would simply make the challenges that more difficult, and the reminders that much more severe.

"During my time as a cook with the guide, I saw something that forever impacted the way I looked at children. On one of the trips, there was a man and a woman from another country. In the evenings we would talk about what it was like where they lived. At the time I did not have children of my own.

"One evening the woman shared with me that the reason they were on their trip was because her husband had become severely depressed. When I asked why, she explained that their only son had left home at the age of nineteen and joined the army. He was killed shortly after that in some faraway country.

"Her husband had become more and more subdued after that happened, and finally doctors had suggested their trip as a possible solution.

"I asked the woman if her son and his father had been close. 'No,' she had replied. 'I believe that is part of what he struggles with. My husband worked very hard, to ensure that our son would go to the best college. He worked six and sometimes seven days a week, and for long hours every day. He didn't like

what he did, but he wanted our son to go to the best school.

"'But it didn't work out that way. When it came time for our son to attend school, he wasn't interested. He and my husband would fight about it all the time. Finally one day our son came into the house and told us that he had joined the army instead. Five months later he was dead.

"'We could never figure out why he made the decision to join the army.'

"'Why did your husband want your son to go to the best college,' I had asked her.

"'To get a good job,' she told me.

"'Did your husband go to a good school, when he was a student?'

"'Yes, he did.'

"'And then he got the job where he worked so hard?'

"'No, not at first, but as our son was getting older, he felt he needed to take that job to make the kind of money our son would need for school.'

"'And he didn't like it?'

"'No, it wasn't the type or work he enjoyed, and as I mentioned, the hours were very long. He did it all so that our son could go to a good school. When our son ended up joining the military instead, it hurt my husband deeply. He went into a deep depression when our son was killed.'

"'Did your son know that his father wanted him to go to a good school so that he could get a good job?'

"'Yes.'"

Ma Ma Gombe looked at me. "That was a very difficult night for me, young Jack. Sometimes we are so close to things that we cannot see them for what they are. In this case, I could see what they could not. Imagine what it must have been like to be their son.

"He would have done anything to avoid going to school, because going to school would have been accepting the responsibility for his father's unhappiness.

"He would have accepted the guilt of being the reason his father was trading his life, for money—the reason his father was at a job he did not like. No one would want to take on that type of guilt for something they never asked for.

"He also saw 'good school' leading to a 'good job' would mean a life just like his father's. Not exactly an ideal future.

"I believe that couple, and their son whom I never met, were actors in my play of life, young Jack. I learned much from their story. Children quickly see through a parent who with their words or actions says 'do what I say, not what I do.'

"'Do not be like me' does not hold much meaning for children, especially when there is no guidance about whom else to be like. I knew that if I were to have children someday, I would

want them to be a success in the way that they would define success for themselves.

"I would want them to fulfill whatever they decided was their Big Five for Life. And I knew that meant I would have to demonstrate for them that I was fulfilling mine."

"And did you?" I asked.

"Yes," she replied. "Whenever I thought about not doing it, I remembered that couple. It always reminded me that one of my greatest roles as a mother was to model a Big Five for Life existence."

"And?" I asked.

"During their lives, my children fulfilled their Big Five for Life many times over, young Jack. And in doing so, they fulfilled one of my own Big Five for Life."

# 20

The next day when we were walking I said, "I feel bad for Epelpo."

"He is on his own journey, young Jack. Epelpo cannot fulfill what he doesn't know. His Who's are all around him but he can't see them because he doesn't know his Big Five for Life. And those around him cannot help, because they do not know what he truly wants to do, see, or experience."

"Maybe he just doesn't know how to get started," I said.

Ma Ma Gombe laughed. "You have a very kind heart, young Jack. That will serve you well in your life. I'm afraid Epelpo knows, he just does not do."

"How can you be so sure, Ma Ma Gombe?"

She laughed again. "I have known Epelpo for many, many years. With him, it is always the same. He does not believe that simple can be powerful, so he tries to make things complex. Then when they are complex enough, he becomes afraid to try them. Achieving your Big Five for Life is not hard, young Jack."

"I almost got killed by poachers trying to achieve part of mine," I said.

"But you did not get killed," she replied. "And if you would have, you would simply have gone on to whatever is next. Having seen the elephants, would you exchange a life *with* that experience, but which ended there, for a life in which you never had that experience?"

I paused. "That's a big question, Ma Ma Gombe."

"Not really, young Jack. If your Big Five for Life are really *your* Big Five for Life, then the success of your existence depends on whether or not you do, see, or experience them."

"Then no," I replied. "I wouldn't take a longer life if it meant I had to give up my Big Five for Life."

"I would not either," she said. "There are no guarantees on how long our own play lasts. While I have never desired to end mine early, it also never made sense to me that I should leave out the best parts, just in case that might make the play last longer.

"Which brings us back to what I said. Achieving your Big Five for Life is not hard. It is simply a matter of knowing what they are, and why you want to achieve them. Then you find your Who's and decide which of them you want to imitate. And then you do, see, or experience whatever is on your list.

"Never confuse simplicity with power, young Jack. Remember what Archimedes said?"

I look at her surprised.

"Do not be surprised," she commented. "I have read much in my days. Archimedes talked about power, and he said, 'Give me a lever long enough and a fulcrum upon which to place it, and I can move the world.'

"A lever is nothing more than a stick, young Jack, and a fulcrum is nothing more than a rock. It does not get much simpler than a stick and a rock, but that does not mean when used correctly they are not powerful. That simple invention changed the world.

"And with the same simplicity, the Big Five for Life changes people's individual worlds. It gives them direction and focus. It enables them to have a successful life as they individually have defined success.

"No, young Jack, it is not that Epelpo does not know. He simply does not do."

# 21

"Ma Ma Gombe, how did you teach your children about the Big Five for Life?" I asked.

She stopped walking. "I showed them this," she said and indicated the sweeping landscape in front of us. "I showed them the way the sky seems to go on forever, and I showed them how each mountain and tree and animal is unique and intriguing. This is our playground. From the moment they were born I told them that the world was theirs and they could do anything they wanted.

"And I showed them that the world was full of possibilities. Most of us learn to suppress our dreams because we don't know exactly how they can be turned into realities. I taught them to head confidently in the direction of their dreams, and let the world know what they were trying to do, and that those dreams were part of their Big Five for Life.

"I taught them that even if they did not know exactly what they wanted, to start down the path of what they thought they

wanted. And when they did that, their Who's showed up everywhere for them.

"Not every Who ended up being the right Who, but my children learned something from every one of them, even if it was learning that they did not want to imitate the ways of that person. Sometimes learning what you don't want is as powerful as learning what you do.

"My children were just toddlers when they first experienced all of this, and when it was successful, they did it again, and again, until there was no reason not to. Success breeds success, young Jack. They also saw how I embraced it in my own life, and how it helped all of us. They never learned *not to* follow their dreams."

"They were very lucky to have you as a mother," I said.

"I was lucky to have *them*," Ma Ma Gombe replied. "I never imagined that they could have brought me the level of joy they did… I was lucky to have them."

Ma Ma Gombe looked at me. Her small wrinkled face stared into mine. "Are you struggling to find the rest of your Big Five for Life, young Jack?"

I shrugged, "Sort of. I'm not too concerned about it because this one is going so well, but it does cross my mind now and again. I wonder if my Who's are all around me but I don't know they are there because I don't know the rest of my Big Five for

Life."

"Think of it as a game, young Jack. If you were free to do anything in your life, what would it be? If money, time, skills, and any barrier that you can imagine were not there, what are the five things that if you did, saw, or experienced them, you could die feeling that your life was a success?

"And if that does not help you, start from the opposite side. Perhaps in Epelpo's case if he thought of all the things he was doing now that he doesn't like, and asked himself why he doesn't like them, he would uncover what he truly wants.

"Perhaps if he said that he would not tend to his goats and you asked him why, he would say because he wants more freedom. And if you asked him what he would do with his freedom, he might say that he would spend time with his family.

"And if you asked him why he would spend more time with his family, he may say that they are his greatest joy and that he wants to give them something to show them they are his greatest joy.

"And perhaps he would discover that the greatest gift he could give them, to show how much they mean to him, is for him to be happy. And the second greatest gift would be for him to spend more time with them, especially when he is happy.

"Perhaps by uncovering what he does not want, he would uncover what he does."

# 22

As springtime turned to summer during our journey, the land in which Ma Ma Gombe and I were walking reflected the severe heat of the sunny days. The ground was dusty and dry and great cracks formed in the soil. The green grasses of spring had long become bright yellow as they dried in the sun each day.

We had descended from the mountains and were making our way across a long savannah. I could not see an end to it, but Ma Ma Gombe assured me that more mountains lay on the other side.

It was here that the lions found us.

We had been walking for many days when I noticed that Ma Ma Gombe appeared to be even more aware than usual of each movement around us. The grass would bend a particular way and she would stop and wait. A bird would call out from behind us and she would turn to watch it for many minutes. I thought she was demonstrating what she loved to remind me about—"Enjoy each step, young Jack, for in every moment there

is something to learn."

In this particular case, there was definitely something to learn.

As the sun reached its peak and blazed down upon us, Ma Ma Gombe said, as if commenting about nothing in particular, "We are being stalked by lions, young Jack."

I instantly turned and looked behind us. All I saw was tall pockets of grass.

"They are staying well behind us," she said. "It is possible they are just curious. It is also possible they are hungry. In the summer when the land becomes dry, many of the animals move on and it is harder for the lions to find prey."

"Are you sure we're being followed?" I asked.

"Yes, I am sure."

"What will they do?" I asked. "Will they attack us?"

"It is possible," she said. "Lions have attacked humans before, although they much prefer antelope."

"What should we do?" I asked.

"Try not to look like an antelope."

# 23

By mid-afternoon we had made our way to a heavy thicket of Acacia trees. Acacia trees are a demonstration of the ongoing battle for survival that exists in nature. In a place where green leaves and water-filled branches are sought by so many animals, the Acacia has evolved giant thorns along its branches as a way to deter the plant-eating animals from destroying it.

Ma Ma Gombe began dragging a large branch that had fallen from one of the trees.

"The lions are getting closer," she said. "I do not think they are just curious anymore. Find as many branches as you can like this, and bring them to me. And hurry, young Jack. We do not have time to waste."

My heart was racing as I dragged branch after branch to Ma Ma Gombe. Each time I turned I expected to see a lion poised to leap at me. The thorns were cutting my hands as I brought them from the thicket, but I didn't care. I knew they were nothing compared to what a lion's claws would do.

There was a rumble in the distance. I looked up and saw dark clouds forming on the far horizon. I moved even faster to find more branches.

With each piece I dragged to her, Ma Ma Gombe was forming a small shelter of thorn-laden branches. She arranged a circular base first, and then piled the branches higher and higher, leaving one spot where I could come in. I brought yet another branch to her, and as I turned to go back to the thicket, she said, "That will have to do, young Jack."

"It's ok, Ma Ma Gombe," I said and started to turn. "I can do it, there are still more branches."

"Young Jack!"

It was the sharpness with which she said my name that caused the hair on the back of my neck to stand up. In all our months of travels, Ma Ma Gombe had never raised her voice to me or anyone else.

"Come into the shelter, young Jack," she said quietly. "Right now."

I turned to look at the Acacia thicket. A full-grown lioness was standing in front of it. She was facing me and her ears were pinned back to her head. Her tail was slowly swishing back and forth.

"Right now," Ma Ma Gombe said again. "And do not make any sudden movements."

I inched my way to the opening. The base branch was almost three feet high. I slowly stepped over it, never taking my eyes off the lioness. I could feel the thorns cutting the back of my legs as I made my way in. Ma Ma Gombe moved me to the back of the enclosure and quickly piled three branches in the space where I had entered. We were now inside a circle of thorns.

"What do we do now?" I asked.

"We wait."

"For what?"

"That depends on the universe," she replied.

There was a rustle in the grass on the other side of our enclosure. A second lioness stepped out. They were both less than twenty feet from us. I could see their muscles stretch taut across their shoulders as they moved. They appeared to be evaluating the situation. Then they both sat down and watched us. They were waiting.

I remembered how I had read that a lion's jaw has five times the crushing power of a human jaw.

I looked at Ma Ma Gombe. "What should we do?"

"Enjoy them, young Jack."

"Enjoy them? Ma Ma Gombe, we are trapped in the middle of a little thorn hut out on the savannah and we have two lions sitting twenty feet away."

"Apparently you have not seen the male yet," she replied, and

nodded her head toward the thicket.

I turned and looked. A full-grown male lion was standing and looking at us. His giant mane was blowing softly in the breeze. As he stood there, his muscles rippled from his shoulders along the length of his entire body. His tail was slowly moving back and forth.

"What should we do?" I asked again.

"Enjoy the moment, young Jack. This is what you came to Africa for, is it not? Most people go their whole lives without ever seeing a lion. Here you are where seeing a lion is part of your Big Five for Life, and you have three of them in front of you. Enjoy them."

"I can't," I said. "I'm terrified." And I was. My whole body was shaking and my mind raced, trying to come up with a solution for getting us out of the enclosure and away from the lions.

Ma Ma Gombe put her hand on my shoulder. "When you have done all you can, young Jack, you must detach from the outcome."

"I don't want to die, Ma Ma Gombe," I said.

"And neither do I," she replied. "We have done all we can. There is nothing else you or I can do right now."

"But if we had taken a different path," I said, "or maybe we should have…"

Ma Ma Gombe touched my shoulder again. "Young Jack, I

know you are afraid. But looking back will not do you any good. When you are faced with a challenge in life, and you have done all you possibly can to overcome it, then you must detach from what happens next. It does no good to worry about what may happen in the future, and it does no good to worry about what you did in the past. In those moments—this moment—you must just be, and let the universe do what it will."

I looked at Ma Ma Gombe. I saw the calm in her eyes and the kindness in her face.

"You told me you have dreamed of seeing these animals since you were a child," she said. "This is your chance. See them."

I looked out at the lions. The male was still standing near the thicket and one of the females had sat down next to him. They were truly spectacular. They were so close that I could see the tiny insects buzzing around their heads. I could see each whisker on their faces. I could also see their giant claws each time they stretched, and their mouths full of teeth each time they yawned.

And yet, in that moment, a calmness descended upon me.

"What will happen, will happen," Ma Ma Gombe said. "Enjoy this moment while it is here."

# 24

I awoke with a start. "Where am I?" I thought. "I was having a dream. There were lions…"

I felt a sharp pain in my shoulder and recoiled from it. It was a thorn. It hadn't been a dream. I was in the middle of the little thorn enclosure.

"I must have fallen asleep," I thought.

I had watched the lions for hours. Once the calmness settled over me and I detached from the outcome, I had sat and marveled at them.

I turned suddenly, "Ma Ma Gombe! Where was Ma Ma Gombe?"

The enclosure was empty. As I looked, I realized that one section of it was pulled away and the branches were strewn about. Ma Ma Gombe was gone.

I sat paralyzed. "They took her," I thought. "The lions took her and I never even heard it." My body wanted to move, but I didn't know what to do, or where to go.

I saw movement in the grass on the edge of the thicket. "They're back for me," I thought. I scrambled to my feet and began trying to close the section of the enclosure that had been pulled away.

I looked up to see if the lions were charging. Instead, there was Ma Ma Gombe smiling at me.

"Have you become attached to our little hut, young Jack?" she yelled. "Come out, there is much to see in the world."

# 25

"I thought you were dead," I said and wrapped my arms around Ma Ma Gombe. "I thought they had taken you."

She laughed, "No, the universe has not taken, the universe has provided.

"Come," she said. "I have something to show you. The storm that was on the horizon yesterday afternoon must have brought them this way."

We walked for several minutes and then Ma Ma Gombe stopped. "Look, young Jack," she said. "Look at one of nature's greatest wonders."

We were on the edge of a section of the savannah that began a slow gradual descent. And for as far as I could see, the land was covered with slow-moving animals.

"Wildebeest," Ma Ma Gombe said. "It is the great migration. Each year during the dry season they make their journey to try and find greener fields. The timing of their arrival here was very lucky for us."

There were hundreds of thousands of them, all slowly walking and grazing. The closest were no more than fifty feet away. Intermixed with the wildebeest were zebras and gazelles. I stood transfixed watching them.

"This is part of the great circle, young Jack. These animals will slowly cover almost two thousand miles as they search for food and water. And during their journey thousands of little ones will be born."

"Is this why the lions didn't attack us?" I asked.

"Yes," she replied. "After you fell asleep, they stayed where they were. I thought they would try to attack during the night. Then as the sun was about to set, they began to sniff the air. Every few minutes they would sniff again. Then suddenly they were gone. They had picked up the scent of the wildebeest."

I looked out at the horizon.

"Try not to look like an antelope, and try not to smell like a wildebeest," I said.

Ma Ma Gombe laughed. "You are learning, young Jack, you are learning."

We both looked out across the plains. "Spectacular," I said. "Absolutely spectacular."

Ma Ma Gombe patted my shoulder. "Fulfilling your Big Five for Life always is, young Jack."

We stayed on the edge of the wildebeest herd for many days,

and in those days I gained a greater appreciation for what Ma Ma Gombe meant when she said all things are connected.

At different intervals we saw lions, cheetah, leopards, and hyenas make attacks on the wildebeest.

"They take the old and the weak," Ma Ma Gombe explained. "Without them, the herd would grow too large and destroy the land. At the same time, the wildebeest, gazelles and zebras that survive, will eat the taller grass, giving the young greener sprouts a chance to grow.

"If that did not occur, the tall grass would become too dry and be more likely to burn from the lighting. What the animals leave behind, the dung beetles put beneath the soil and it enriches the ground, helping the new seeds to sprout.

"It is all connected. Each animal and insect and plant exists for a reason."

"What about us?" I asked. "Why are we here?"

"I believe that is for each of us to decide," she said. "We can choose to exist for a reason, such as to fulfill our Big Five for Life. And in that case, I believe the universe is always there to help us along the way. Or we can choose to just exist. The choice is ours."

"Do you think many people choose to *just exist*?" I asked.

"I have seen many things in my life, young Jack. I have met many people. One thing I have learned is that sometimes not

choosing is the same as choosing. People will talk about what they want, and sometimes they even ask for it. But I think maybe the universe is not just listening, it is listening and watching."

"You and I could have arrived at the Acacia thicket and sat on the ground and wished that the lions would not eat us. We could have asked the universe to provide us with shelter to keep the lions away. But I think if that is all we had done, we would have been eaten by now.

"I believe it is good to ask the universe for help as we fulfill our Big Five for Life, but I think we must demonstrate to the universe how much it means to us. And we do that by taking part in our own success.

"We did not bring the wildebeest here, but if we had not gathered the Acacia branches and did our part to keep the lions away, perhaps the universe would have sent the wildebeest somewhere else last night."

# 26

"Where to now, Ma Ma Gombe?" I asked.

After weeks of walking, we had left the wildebeest and the savannah behind and were at the base of a new stretch of mountains.

"I think perhaps we need to get you to a doctor, young Jack. I do not like the way your wound looks."

A week earlier I had cut my hand while preparing firewood, and it was not healing very quickly.

"It's not that bad, Ma Ma Gombe."

"It is bad enough. This way."

She began to walk toward the mountains. "Ma Ma Gombe, how is it that you know these regions so well? We spent weeks crossing a savannah that seemed to stretch on forever, and yet as soon as it ends, you know where you are."

"I try to fill my mind with what is important to me, young Jack. When you don't clutter it full of useless things there is plenty of room in your brain for what matters to you. I have

been here many times in my life. Each time I come back it is easier to remember and easier to find.

"You should be happy you weren't with me the first time. I wandered for days before finally figuring it out. But with each time that you try something, you get better. Almost everyone wanders a little off course from time to time. You just have to make sure you don't give up.

"Going left when you should go right is only a problem if you never turn around, or if you completely stop walking. We humans seem to be the only animals who struggle with this," she said.

"The monkeys will taste different fruits and learn which ones are good and which ones are not. They don't stop eating just because they find a fruit that looks like it is edible but isn't. And they don't keep eating the same non-edible fruit and hoping that it will suddenly be good to eat.

"When the giraffe are walking in the savannah and they find fire caused by the lightning, they do not continue into the fire. Nor do they sit down and complain that the fire is there, or blame someone else because they can't get to their favorite trees. They simply find another way.

"And each time they learn something new, they remember it."

# 27

When we arrived at the clinic, Ma Ma Gombe and I were greeted by a white-haired man named Kilali.

"Hello, Ma Ma Gombe," he said warmly as they hugged. "What brings you all the way out here?"

"My young friend and I are pursuing our Big Five for Life," she said, "and he has cut himself. I did all that I could, but it is not working."

"What did you try?" he asked.

For the next ten minutes, Kilali and Ma Ma Gombe discussed what she had done to try to heal my wound. I realized that I was watching exactly what Ma Ma Gombe had described with the animals. She had tried to heal me, but it wasn't working. So she brought me to Kilali to try something new.

Along the way, she and I were learning new things, which we would now know for the rest of our lives.

"What you did would normally work, Ma Ma Gombe," Kilali said. "But because the drought has been so severe, those

herbs do not have the healing power they normally do. What we have found instead, is that…"

And so it went. Ma Ma Gombe was not upset or embarrassed that she didn't know how to cure me. She asked Kilali many questions and treated the experience as a great learning opportunity. "She is always finding her Who's," I thought to myself. "She is always learning."

That evening we stayed with Kilali. "How do you know Ma Ma Gombe?" I asked him.

He smiled, "Ma Ma Gombe is the reason I am a doctor."

"That is not true, Kilali," she replied and patted his arm. "You are a doctor because of all the hard work you did to become a doctor."

"Well then, Ma Ma Gombe is responsible for helping me find the way to become a doctor," Kilali said. "When I was a boy, my teachers thought I possessed the aptitude to continue my studies. I loved the sciences and they could not provide me with enough new books, I read them so fast. But my family was very poor, and my father did not know how he could afford to send me to the next level of school.

"One day Ma Ma Gombe came into our village and when my father heard her teaching the children about the Big Five for Life, he came up to her and asked if she could help him fulfill one of his. When she asked him what he needed, he said he needed a job

cutting wood."

"I thought it was an odd request," Ma Ma Gombe interjected. "With all that one could choose, here was a man wanting a job cutting wood as one of his Big Five for Life. So I asked him why he wanted that. 'Not that I am judging you,' I explained to him. For after all, it was his list and he could put on it what he wished, but I was curious.

"He told me he wanted the job because he had heard wood cutters could make much money. So I asked him why he wanted the money. It was then that tears came to his eyes, and he explained how he wanted Kilali to have the chance to go to school, but he could not afford to send him."

"My father was a very proud man," Kilali commented.

"And a very good man," Ma Ma Gombe added. "I have never seen a father with greater love for his son."

"I take it you helped him get the job?" I asked Ma Ma Gombe.

"No, young Jack, and there is a very valuable lesson in this for you. When you are figuring out your Big Five for Life, it is important to ask yourself *why* you have chosen those items. Having a job as a wood cutter was not truly part of Kilali's father's Big Five for Life.

"It was simply the way he saw of getting to what he really wanted, which was somehow enabling his son to continue going to school.

"The people whom I contacted and talked to about Kilali going to school, were very different than the people I would have talked to if I was truly trying to get Kilali's father a job as a wood cutter.

"The universe and those around us will help us get what we ask for with our Big Five for Life. So it is very important that we ask for what we truly want."

I turned to Kilali. "Did your father ever get to see you take care of patients, Kilali?"

"Oh yes," Kilali said and laughed. "He worked here in the clinic for many years before he passed away…"

Kilali paused and a tear rolled down his face. He gently brushed it to the side. "You have never seen such a diligent worker. I used to laugh every time, because the first thing he did after he greeted people was to tell them that they were in very good hands, that his son was a very good doctor."

"I'm sure he was very proud that you were his son," I said.

"He was, and I was proud that he was my father."

# 28

On the third day of our stay with Kilali, Ma Ma Gombe told me she had something special for me to see.

"What is it?" I asked.

"Tonight you are going to witness your first Talimpopo," she said.

"What's that?"

"It is a celebration of the pursuit of the Big Five for Life. And it is a quick way to find your Who's."

In the late afternoon, people began to gather in the courtyard in front of the clinic. Before long, the entire area was very crowded.

"It seems like the whole village is here," I said to Ma Ma Gombe.

"They are," she replied.

"Why?" I asked.

"You will see. And perhaps participate too."

A few minutes later, a young woman walked to the front

of the crowd. People began applauding and cheering as she ascended to the top of the three steps leading into the clinic. She was about 14 years old and was smiling.

"Thank you," she said. "My name is Lalamba. Thank you for your enthusiasm, your excitement, and thank you in advance for your help. I am about to begin pursuing my Big Five for Life, and I do not know exactly where to begin. I would like to explain to you what they are, and if you can help me, I would like to hear what you have to say."

What happened over the next three hours was nothing short of miraculous. At the start, Lalamba explained each of her Big Five for Life, and why she had chosen them. Then she asked the group to help her figure out the best way to do, see, and experience them. And the group did. Each person, no matter their age, or role in the village, was encouraged to offer their ideas. Some of the best ones came from the young children.

"They are the most creative," Ma Ma Gombe commented. "They see all that can be, instead of all that cannot."

After an idea was stated, it quickly grew in strength, because of the efforts of the entire group. From the initial statement, the idea was enhanced immediately by someone else, and then again by someone else, and then again, so that within minutes it had gone from a dream to a possibility. With each improvement, the crowd cheered and clapped, and encouraged each other on.

"There is much power in the Talimpopo," Ma Ma Gombe said as we watched the events unfold. "Through the collective effort of the many, Lalamba will move much faster towards her Big Five for Life.

"You see, young Jack, we each view the world differently because of our experiences. When the lion chases the wildebeest and the vulture to the edge of the cliff, it is the same cliff. But where the wildebeest sees death at the edge, the vulture sees freedom.

"An infection from an Acacia tree thorn can be deadly to the person who does not know how to fix it, but to a skilled doctor the cure is as simple as applying the right salve.

"The purpose of the Talimpopo is to help someone see what they did not use to see—to open their eyes to new possibilities. And in the process, each person who participates gains as well."

"What do you mean?"

"Lalamba is not the only one who will remember what was said here tonight. As each idea evolves and improves for her, each person is also thinking about how what they hear can help them with their own Big Five for Life. And there is more.

"Look at the people. Do you see the joy they get from help-ing her? No matter how long it takes, or where she is, as they hear of how Lalamba is succeeding, each person here will take great joy in knowing that they helped her along the way. Her

success is their success."

As the people assisted Lalamba with each of her Big Five for Life, they also started to draw linkages between them. Where some ideas had come to impasses before, they now moved beyond the impasse because of something in one of her other Big Five for Life.

"Our Big Five for Life are all connected," Ma Ma Gombe said. "The man who wants to be the best father possible and at the same time wants to see the world, does both by taking his son with him on a journey. And in the process, both their eyes are opened."

When the evening had ended, and the other people had gone home, I sat with Ma Ma Gombe on the clinic steps.

"That was fascinating," I said.

"I thought you would find it to be, young Jack. Perhaps there is a Talimpopo somewhere in your future. Perhaps there will be many Talimpopos in your future. What you saw tonight was Lalamba's first, but it is unlikely that it will be her last. Whenever she is stuck she will ask for assistance again. The same is possible for you."

"I don't think the people where I live know what a Talimpopo is, Ma Ma Gombe."

"Then I suppose you will have to teach them, young Jack."

# 29

I awoke at dawn to the sound of jaws crunching next to my head. I jerked my body to the side and rolled. As I started to get up, I found myself staring into giant dark eyes on opposite sides of a giant dark head.

"Easy, young Jack," Ma Ma Gombe said, in a soft calm voice. "Make no sudden movements. They do not like sudden movements." Her fingers locked around my arm and slowly pulled me away from the massive head.

The night before, Ma Ma Gombe and I had camped in a grassy valley that at the time appeared empty except for us.

"What is that?" I asked.

"African Buffalo," she replied. "You are in the midst of the last of your African Big Five."

She eased me into a standing position.

"They came in while we were sleeping," she said. "I woke just a few moments before you did."

The animal that I had just encountered was only five feet away, and Ma Ma Gombe was slowly backing us away from it. It had massive dark black horns that curved majestically on each side of its head, and it was enormous.

"They weigh almost eighteen hundred pounds," Ma Ma Gombe said, "and their horns can be deadly. For the most part they are very docile, but they do not like to be startled. I think he is as surprised to see us as we are to see him."

"Will he charge?" I asked.

"Not unless we attack him first. And that is something you never want to do with an African buffalo. An elephant or rhinoceros can be very dangerous because of their sheer size, but they will often make fake charges and then back off. There is no backing off for one of these. When something attacks them, they will attack back until they either kill the attacker, or the attacker kills them."

"Good to know," I replied. "What do we do now?"

"We walk away," she said. "Which means we are going to have to walk through them."

"Them?"

Up to that point I had been staring at the buffalo in front of us. I took my eyes off it for a second and glanced around. We were in the middle of a herd of buffalo. There must have been close to a thousand of them and they were everywhere.

"This is a very large group," Ma Ma Gombe commented. "It is a miracle they did not accidentally step on us while we were sleeping."

"And it will be a miracle if we make it out of here," I replied.

"One step at a time, young Jack. No matter how we may wish, it is not possible to take it any faster than that. If we run we will startle them. Can you take one step?"

"Yes."

"Then do that, and then do it again. And keep doing it until we are outside of the herd."

At first I was very afraid. But with each step, the journey out became easier. Soon I came to the realization that it was less dangerous than I had thought. As long as we moved slowly and did not startle the buffalo, they were content to eat the grass and issue an occasional bellow.

I began to focus on the animals, and appreciate the amazing experience that I was in the middle of. The more I did that, the more my fear disappeared.

When we had made our way through the last of the buffalo, we climbed up a small hill and sat beneath one of the shade trees.

"It was not as bad as you thought it would be, was it, young Jack? Such is often the case with life. We cannot climb to the

top of the mountain by wishing it were so. And no matter how afraid of the height we may be, we cannot get down the mountain by wishing it were so. But if we simply start on the path, and take it one step at a time, there is nowhere we cannot get to."

# 30

That evening, Ma Ma Gombe and I sat by the fire. As she had throughout our travels, Ma Ma Gombe pointed out the constellations and had me name them for her and recite back what they meant, and how you could use them to figure out where you were. There is nothing quite like the stars of an African night.

I explained to her that there were more than one hundred billion stars just in our galaxy, and that the most we were probably able to see with our eyes was just three thousand.

As the last embers of the fire were burning down, Ma Ma Gombe turned to me.

"Young Jack, we have traveled far, you and I. It was many months ago when we first met and sat upon the plateau looking out at the zebras. The buffalo today were the last of the Big Five that you came to Africa to see. There were the elephants at Adoo, the leopard and rhinoceros at the cliff, the lions in the savannah, and today the buffalo."

"Not to mention the zebras, gazelles, kudu, impala, wilde-beest, giraffes, and all the others," I said.

"Yes, there have been many others," she replied. "Has it been what you expected?"

I put my hand on her arm. "Much more, Ma Ma Gombe. It has been much more than I ever hoped for."

"I am glad, young Jack."

Ma Ma Gombe paused for a while. "Young Jack, I want to ask you a favor, and I want you to promise me that you will only say yes if your heart truly tells you to."

"What is it, Ma Ma Gombe?"

"I have lived very long, and I have done much in my life. There are many things that I have put on my Big Five for Life list, and then completed. I told you when we met that there is one final thing on my list though. One place I would like to go. And if your heart tells you to, I would like you to go there with me."

"The birthplace of all?"

"Yes, young Jack, the birthplace of all."

"Where is it, Ma Ma Gombe?"

"I do not know exactly. That will be part of the adventure. One of the greatest skills you can have when you are trying to fulfill your Big Five for Life is the willingness to ask others for help. We will need to do that often if we are to find this place.

"I told you that when I was a very young girl my grandfather used to tell me about his visit there. He said it was a place where you could see the earth be born, and then watch the world go to sleep, a place so beautiful that words cannot describe it."

"I would like to see that, Ma Ma Gombe," I said. "I would like to go there with you."

Ma Ma Gombe looked at me. "Thank you, young Jack. I would like that too."

# 31

It took us three months to find the birthplace of all. Many times we would walk for days only to find out that we needed to go in the opposite direction. But we persisted on. I realized as we dealt with those setbacks how important a Who was.

When you know something exists, or that it is possible to do, see, or experience it, the delays are nothing more than just that. We knew that Ma Ma Gombe's grandfather had been to the birthplace of all, so we knew it was possible for us to go there. Because of that, we did not doubt that we would succeed. It was simply a matter of time and perseverance.

On a rainy and foggy morning, we were walking through a deep gorge when Ma Ma Gombe stopped and picked up a rock. She brushed off the dirt, and turned it over in her hand a few times. Her eyes lit up.

"We are close, young Jack," she said and handed me the rock.

I took it and turned it over. It was the top part of a human skull, but it was petrified, like a rock.

"When my grandfather used to tell me about this place, he told me that it was home to our oldest ancestors," she said. "He told me that they had been here so long ago, that their bones had turned to stone. He said that you could see the valley where the bones were, from the birthplace of all."

I looked around. It was so foggy that we couldn't see more than a few hundred feet in any direction.

"What should we do?" I asked.

"Wait."

The words had barely escaped her lips, when the sun began to appear through the fog. With each passing minute, the world around us began to materialize.

"This way," Ma Ma Gombe said, and began walking quickly.

"How do you know?"

"Because he told me."

With the fog it had been impossible to see, but with each step that we took forward, I realized that we were at the base of a large plateau. In front of us was a long winding trail that looked like it made its way up the side of the cliff.

# 32

After almost a full day of climbing, we arrived at the top of the plateau. When we did, I saw that it was a long thin piece of land, dense with trees and hundreds of feet above the rest of the terrain.

As we made our way through the woods, the vegetation suddenly ended, and in front of us was a stretch of solid flat rock that extended for about 50 feet. There were no trees except for a single old one growing at the very end of the plateau.

"This is it," Ma Ma Gombe said. "This is what he told me it would be like."

"Look at that tree," I said. The trunk was twisted and worn and looked like it had been battling for all eternity to earn its spot on that rock. "It must be…"

"Very old," Ma Ma Gombe said, almost to herself. "And very strong to have survived out here for so long."

Despite its age, the tree had a broad, green canopy, and we sat beneath it and looked at what lay below. To the west

was savannah. Long, tall elephant grass waved in the sun and dominated the landscape. It was interrupted by the occasional Baobab and other trees.

The savannah was full of animals. Herds of zebra and gazelle grazed among the grasses and giant giraffe stretched their necks to the farthest reaches of the tall trees. We could see elephants and rhinoceros in the distance.

To the east, a river wound its way through dark green forests and onto stretches of granite rocks where groups of hippopotamus played in the deep water pools. Large crocodiles sat open-mouthed on the river banks, and huge flocks of white and pink birds flew in formation over the canopy of the forest.

The air was warm and filled with the sounds of screeching monkeys, bird calls, and the occasional roar of a lion.

It was now late afternoon and the sun was settling low on the horizon. To the east, the river took on the shimmering pink reflection of the sunset, and the forest became a deep vibrant green.

To the west, the sun slowly eased half-way beneath the horizon, leaving behind what I believe must be the most beautiful sunset ever created. As we sat there watching the sky become a brilliant mix of pink, orange, red, and silver, Ma Ma Gombe clasped my hand.

Her rough, gnarled fingers intertwined with mine and she

looked at me with tears in her eyes. "I cannot imagine having missed this," she said softly, and droplets began to roll from the corners of her eyes and down her checks. "It is beautiful, so very beautiful."

# 33

When I woke the next morning, Ma Ma Gombe was not in her usual spot starting up the morning fire. I looked around and spotted her sitting on the edge of the plateau facing the morning sunrise. As I approached, I realized that suddenly she looked very old. It was as if making it here had kept her young, and driven her on, and now that she had fulfilled her last wish, her true age was showing through.

"Good morning, Ma Ma Gombe," I said, as I sat down on the rock next to her.

"Good morning, young Jack," she replied and patted my arm. "Is it not beautiful?" she asked and stretched her hand towards the sun, which was just beginning to show on the horizon. "It is as if the universe is waking. As if she is calling to her creations, 'Open your leaves, open your eyes, open your minds. There is a new day to experience.'"

We sat and watched as the sun rose into the morning sky.

"Thank you, Ma Ma Gombe," I said, and put my arm around

her shoulders. "Thank you for letting me see this with you."

She smiled, and patted me on the knee. "You are welcome, young Jack. Perhaps some day *you* will guide someone here and show them where the universe wakes and goes to sleep."

After a few minutes of silence, where we both watched the earth spring to life, Ma Ma Gombe turned to me.

"Young Jack, I have made a decision. I will not be going back with you. I am going to stay here."

I looked at her, surprised, "What do you mean?"

"I mean that this is where I want to sit for a while," she replied, and smiled at me. "I am a very old woman now. This was the last of my Big Five for Life and now I think it is time for a rest for old Ma Ma Gombe."

I began to protest. "But Ma Ma Gombe, you are not that old. You made it here. You guided me this whole way. I could never have made one tenth of this journey alone. *You* were the strength that got us to this place."

She reached out and touched my arm. "You will be fine, young Jack," she said, and smiled again. "You and I have taught each other much in our many months together. You are no longer a visitor to Africa. Now you are one of her children, and a mother always takes care of her children. You will find your way. Africa will guide you home."

Tears began to roll down my cheeks. "But what about the

students at the school, Ma Ma Gombe, and the people in the villages? What will they do?"

I knew what Ma Ma Gombe was proposing. It wasn't that she wanted to "sit for a while." Ma Ma Gombe was choosing this as her final resting place.

Ma Ma Gombe looked up at me, and with her gnarled fingers she wiped her hand across my face and brushed away the tears.

"Yes," she replied. "This is where my journey will end. You cannot live your life for others, young Jack. The children, the people in the villages, they have their own Big Five for Life to fulfill. My role was to inspire them, and I did the best I could at that. Now it is up to them. Just as it is up to you to fulfill the rest of your Big Five for Life."

"How will I do that without you, Ma Ma Gombe?"

"You won't be without me, young Jack. Just as my grandfather helped guide me here, I will always be there to help guide you on your journey."

That evening as I was preparing to go to sleep, I looked at Ma Ma Gombe sitting on the rocks, staring up at the stars. I walked over to her and as I sat down, she commented, "Over one hundred billion stars you said, young Jack?"

"Yes, Ma Ma Gombe, and that is just our galaxy."

She looked up at the stars again. "I am going to explore them all."

# 34

Ma Ma Gombe died that night. I buried her in the place she had dreamt of seeing for so long, and had finally gotten to visit. I cried the entire time.

I knew it was her time. I knew she was ready to move on, in her way. But I missed her. I missed my friend.

That night, I put out the fire and lay on my back, staring up at the sky. I found the Northern Star, and the Big Dipper, and Orion. I thought of what she had taught me about them. And for just a brief moment I heard Ma Ma Gombe's voice whispering in the wind.

"What are your Big Five for Life, young Jack, and how can I help you fulfill them?"

# Epilogue

It took me over a year to leave Africa after Ma Ma Gombe died. Although in truth, one never really leaves Africa. Once you visit her, she remains a part of your soul forever, no matter where you go.

During my travels back, I gained great clarity about the rest of my Big Five for Life. I had fulfilled the first one of seeing and experiencing the people, geography, and animals of Africa. It was now time to fulfill the rest.

When I first met her, Ma Ma Gombe explained to me that visitors gauged the success of their African safari experience by how many of the Big Five animals they saw. I was determined to succeed in what I considered my own personal life safari. The subsequent journey has been nothing short of amazing.

Every few years, when the pull of Africa grows too strong to ignore, I leave everything behind for a while and I return to the birthplace of all. That is my time for meeting with my old friend, Ma Ma Gombe. Her spirit is forever with me,

and when I am there, I feel like my old friend has clasped her hand in mine, and we are once again watching the world awaken.

"There is a place inside our soul where we hold our greatest wishes. Those wishes are our Big Five for Life," Ma Ma Gombe had once told me. I remember that, and I remember her, always.

# Authors Note

Years ago during a nine-month backpacking trip around the world, my wife and I visited the continent of Africa for the first time. The experience was life-changing. Words cannot do justice to a place so alive with energy, so steeped in history, and so full of mystery and adventure.

You do not just visit Africa and then leave. Instead, you become a part of Africa, and it takes up a permanent residence within you.

While we were there I had some of the most powerful epiphanies of my entire life, and I experienced what I had dreamed of since I was a small child. I experienced the people, the landscape, and the animals of Africa.

Having been there, I cannot imagine going through life without experiencing Africa. I encourage you to visit this amazing continent. Introduce yourself to her people, gaze upon her majestic natural beauty, and see for yourself what it is like to spend a day on the savannah. Your life will be forever enriched.

There is a timelessness to Africa that forever shifts your perspective on what is, and what is not important. You don't want

to miss that. Quite honestly, you want to experience it sooner rather than later, because the benefits of that experience will enhance every day that you are alive on this planet.

As Ma Ma Gombe says, "This is a beautiful playground we have been given."

**Ready to discover and live your**

# BIG FIVE FOR LIFE?

**Join me at my next Big Five for
Life Discovery Workshop.**

**For more information visit
www.thelifesafari.com**

If after reading the story of Jack and Ma Ma Gombe
you feel the urge to experience Africa for yourself,
I encourage you with all my heart to do so.
It is something you will treasure forever.

To that end, let me try and be a Who for you.
On the next group of pages is information to help you
take your Africa dreams and make them a reality.

Step boldly my friend, adventures await.

# Interested in experiencing Africa for yourself?

One of the keys to truly experiencing Africa, is to find people who don't just organize tours there, but who also have their heart there. They love Africa and because of that, they want to introduce others to the wonders that Africa holds.

If you have a calling to visit Africa, I encourage you to contact a great "Who" duo - James Weis and Nicky Glover.

James and Nicky met on safari in Botswana, fell in love, married, and went on to form a company called Eyes on Africa, which specializes in helping people experience Africa.

They are incredibly passionate about what they do and have deep expertise in what Africa has to offer. Nicky is South African and both of them have spent large amounts of time touring and leading people through many parts of Africa.

I've included some additional details about James, Nicky and their company in the next few pages. If you're interested in experiencing Africa, give them a call. Their phone number is 800-457-9575 and their website is www.eyesonafrica.net.

Enjoy the adventure!
John P. Strelecky

**Eyes on Africa**
Travel & Safaris

As the sun sets on the horizon, you sit and
watch a mother zebra and her baby foal
drink from the edge of a water hole.

To your left you see giraffes reaching
with their long necks to eat leaves from
the tallest branches of acacia trees.

To your right, a family of elephants are
slowly moving through the thatch grass.
In the distance you hear a roar as
a lion claims his territory.

This is Africa, and *you* are there.

www.eyesonafrica.net

## About Eyes on Africa

Founders James Weis and Nicky Glover have introduced thousands of travelers to the wonders and beauty of Africa. Their love of what they do is a reflection of what happens when you blend enthusiasm and dedication with your career. Nicky was born and raised in South Africa and has always combined her love of nature and wildlife with her passion for the continent of her birth. Through her years of experience working on the ground with some of the leading Safari Operators in Africa, she has first hand knowledge of the camps and lodges available.

James is an extremely keen and experienced photographer and naturalist, who typically spends 8-10 weeks per year on safari. He also leads exclusive photo safari workshops, combining digital photography instruction with Africa's premier wildlife and safari settings.

## www.eyesonafrica.net

## Begin Your African Adventure

We would be honored to introduce you to the Africa we love. To get started, contact us at the following number for an initial discussion about some of the many African Safari options available.

800-457-9575
Or visit us online at
www.eyesonafrica.net

# About the Author

Following a life changing event when he was thirty-three years old, John was inspired to sit down and tell the story of *The Why Café*, his first book. He had no previous experience or academic training as a writer.

Within a year after its release, word of mouth support from readers had spread the book across the globe—inspiring people on every continent, including Antarctica. It went on to become a #1 Best Seller. John then went on to write *Life Safari* and *The Big Five for Life– Leadership's Greatest Secret*. He coauthored the book *How to be Rich and Happy*. His books have now been translated into twenty-one languages.

Through his writings and appearances on television and radio, John's messages have inspired millions to live life on their terms. He has been honored alongside Oprah Winfrey, Wayne Dyer, Deepak Chopra, and Stephen R. Covey as one of the 100 Most Influential Thought Leaders in the field of leadership and personal development. All of this continues to humble and amaze him.

Since 2004, he has been actively involved with helping individuals discover and live their Big Five for Life. He also trains coaches to do the same for their clients, through his Big Five for Life Coaching Certification Trainings.

When he isn't writing, training or speaking, John spends extensive time fulfilling another part of his Big Five for Life—traveling the world. He and his wife's longest trip was an almost year long backpacking adventure around the globe. He has taken additional extended trips to the Amazon Basin, Yucatan Peninsula, and China.

To learn more about John, or to inquire about his availability for interviews and as a speaker, please visit;

www.thelifesafari.com